D0046071

THE SILENT STARS GO BY

THE SILENT STARS GO BY

SALLY NICHOLLS

WALKER BOOKS

Copyright © 2020 by Sally Nicholls

First US edition 2022
First published by Andersen Press Ltd (UK) 2020

Library of Congress Catalog Card Number 2021953240
ISBN 978-1-5362-2318-7

22 23 24 25 26 27 LBM 10 9 8 7 6 5 4 3 2 1

Printed in Melrose Park, IL, USA

This book was typeset in Goudy Old Style.

Walker Books US
a division of
Candlewick Press
99 Dover Street
Somerville, Massachusetts 02144

www.walkerbooksus.com

Crowshurst Farm Crowshurst
North Yorkshire
9th December 1919

Dear Margot,

 I do not wish to be a millstone round your neck, and if you really would rather have nothing more to do with me, I won't be such an ass as to insist that you uphold your promises or anything beastly like that. But I think it only polite to inform you that I shall be coming home for Christmas and we are likely—in the usual run of things—to find ourselves somewhat in one another's pockets.

 We may no longer be lovers, but I would hate to think we were ever anything but friends. I cannot claim to understand why you chose to ignore my previous communications, but I trust that you have your reasons. I must say, I think you might have the decency to tell me what they are.

 If you have heard any ill of me, please allow me the chance to explain myself. Though I can't imagine what the devil it is you might have heard.

I remain your most obedient etc.

(truly, Margot, I do),

Harry Singer

Margot Allen sat in the corner of the third-class compartment carriage and read this letter for the fifteenth time. Her mother had forwarded it without comment from the vicarage. The wheels of the train went *clackety-clack, clackety-clack* over the tracks, the little steam heater blasted hot air into the compartment, and outside the windows the Vale of York swept past, all gray and dark green beneath the midwinter sky.

Her small hands, in pale, rather worn leather gloves, rested on her skirt, which was the exact blue of her eyes. Her blond hair was perfectly arranged.

The darns in her overcoat were almost—but not quite—invisible.

Margot was nineteen, but right now she felt herself fully forty-five at least.

The letter, like those that had preceded it, remained unanswered.

I trust that you have your reasons . . .

She leaned her head back against the seat.

Clearly things couldn't go on like this. This secret should never have been kept from him. One way or another, they were going to have to face it.

JOCELYN

❖──❖❖❖──❖

THE STATION AT THWAITE WAS A ONE-PLATFORM village halt with a single sad-looking flowerpot and not even a shelter from the wind. Jocelyn was waiting on the platform, and Margot felt a sudden, unexpected rush of love at the sight of her—her hair falling down out of her hat and her hand-me-down coat hanging rather lumpishly at the back. Darling Jos. It was so nice to be somewhere where people loved you.

The sisters embraced. "Hullo!"

"Hullo, yourself. Where's Mother?"

"Presiding over schoolroom tea. Ernest's train got in just after luncheon. You remember what a beastly lot of fuss there always is."

"Heavens, yes."

They exchanged rueful glances.

"You'd think no child had ever been sent away to school before Mother's boys," Margot said. "Stephen home yet?"

"Not till next week. Is that all your things? Father's got the car this afternoon, so we'd better find a porter to take them up to the house."

"Fancy us with a car!" Margot gave her younger sister a real smile. "Oh look—there's a porter there! I say!"

With the suitcases safely handed over, the sisters set off through the village toward home.

⋯•◦✕◦•⋯

HOW LOVELY IT WAS TO BE BACK. EACH TIME, THE feeling of home surprised her: the clear air, so different from the coal smoke of Durham; the dales above the village and the fields below; the particularly Yorkshire scent of frost and sheep-farming countryside. Home.

The vicarage was a rambling early-Victorian affair. It had been built in the days when vicars were expected to produce eight or nine children for the good of the Empire and—Margot's mother often said—had been bleeding its occupants dry ever since. It was a huge, drafty building, forever in a state of general disrepair. The chimneys smoked, the windows rattled, and it was furnished with a mixture of dilapidated odds and ends left behind by previous vicars and their families. It was always cold, even in the middle of summer. In winter, ice froze in the bedroom jugs and on the windowpanes, and everyone had chilblains despite untold layers of woolen underwear and petticoats. Four children still at home, and the perpetual impossibility of finding servants, on top of her duties as the vicar's wife, meant their mother lived in a state of permanent exhaustion. The garden was a tangled wilderness of fruit trees, chickens, and scraggly vegetables.

The Allen children were accepted eccentrics, bright, bookish, and insular. Their childhood had been one of private games and fierce alliances. Margot had always been the odd one out. While her siblings were angular and awkward and—why not say it?—plain, Margot was something of a beauty. This, in a family that considered humility to be next to godliness, was not always an advantage. Margot was not stupid—none of the Allen children were—but she'd had a reputation as "difficult" from early childhood.

This sense of difference had played out, Margot remembered, as an intense determination for something that was "hers." Toys in the Allen nursery were generally held communally, clothes and other possessions were handed down to younger siblings, and a common front was expected to be presented. Family honor was so important that Margot had once grumbled that anyone would think they were a duke's children instead of a clergyman's.

To be different was . . . not exactly frowned upon, but definitely considered "up yourself." "She's no better than she ought to be" was one of Nanny's greatest slurs. If a vicarage child did well at something—and they generally were somewhere near the top of their classes—they were expected not to make a fuss of it, to say thank you for any praise, and to politely change the subject. Demurring "Oh, I'm rotten at Latin, really" was considered "affected," but boasting was considered "stuck-up" and was even worse. Margot could still remember bouncing home aged nine, delighted because a stranger in the street had described her as "a most striking child." She had been firmly sat upon by her older brother, Stephen, and told by her father to "Consider the lilies of the field."

"The ones that toil not, neither do they spin?" she'd said. "Does that mean I'm excused chores?"

Margot knew she was considered stuck-up. She had been christened Margaret, a name she had always hated, and had changed it to Margot at fourteen, refusing to answer to Margaret until her family had had to admit defeat. She knew Stephen and Jocelyn and even Ruth had always considered her something of an ass. None of them cared about how they looked. But Margot had always loved beautiful things. When the Hendersons at the manor house would bring weekend guests to church, she would sit and stare at their dresses. There was never enough money to go around in the vicarage. Margot had spent her childhood in hand-me-downs from various cousins and homemade creations run up on the Singer sewing machine by Mother.

She had an eye for color and line, and a determination to look good. Even now, after all her troubles, she still kept her hair carefully smoothed back, her eyebrows plucked, her fingernails manicured.

Nowadays, that dissatisfied, out-of-place girl seemed very long ago and far away. Nowadays, Margot wasn't difficult. She wasn't much of anything, really. Sometimes she felt as though all her personality and contrariness had been washed away, leaving something limp and wet-raggish and spinsterish, if you could be such a thing at nineteen.

Or perhaps she had just grown up.

As a child, she had often wondered if she were a foundling, or perhaps swapped at birth. It would be just like her father to take on a villager's child in need of a home. Except, of course, Margot's mother wouldn't be a villager, really—she would be an earl's daughter fleeing disgrace. Meeting her father by chance on her desperate flight, she had been so struck by his goodness, she'd sworn him to secrecy. And now her brothers had all been killed, and the family was coming to find their one true heir . . .

It was a childish enough story, and of course she had known it wasn't really true. She had the look of her grandmother anyway, and the same fair hair as Stephen and Ernest (Jocelyn and Ruth tended more to mouse). But she could still remember the awfulness of feeling so out of favor, so much the odd one out. Margot supposed that her mother loved her. But she had never been entirely sure that she *liked* her.

At least her mother liked James. Margot was grateful for that every . . . well, every time she reminded herself to be, which was less often than she ought. Her mother loved James. Though how anyone could do anything *but* love him!

"How's James?" she said abruptly to Jocelyn.

Jocelyn, who had been waiting for this, gave a private grimace.

"He's well. You'll see—we're to join them for nursery tea. He's talking so much more than when you saw him at half term!"

"And he's . . ." Margot knew she was being a dope, but she said it anyway, as she always did. "He's happy?"

"Yes, he's happy." Jocelyn looked at her sister. "He's a very happy child, Margot. Mother and Father treat him just the same as they do Ruth and Ernest. You don't need me to tell you that."

Margot stiffened.

"I do, though, don't I?" she said. "That's the whole problem."

JAMES

————✦————

"MARGOT! MARGOT'S HOME!"

Ruth and Ernest came clattering down the stairs and flung themselves on their sister with an enthusiasm that Margot knew would not last the evening. Eleven-year-old Ruth had shot up since half term—her thin braids bounced around her face as she capered in the hallway. Ernest looked taller too and somehow older than his eight years, impossibly neat in his gray flannel suit.

He said, "Hullo, Margot." A perfect little stolid Englishman.

"Did you get my letter?" said Ruth. "I've decided what I'm going to be when I grow up." She hopped up and down. "I'm going to be a detective inspector and solve crimes. Women can be policemen now, did you know? Ernest and

I are going to practice this holiday, only we haven't got a mystery to solve yet. You don't know one, do you?"

"That would be telling," said Margot. There was, of course, a mystery—well, not a mystery exactly, but a family secret hiding right under Ruth's nose. But Margot had no intention of telling her about it.

"Hullo, darling," said Margot's mother, kissing her. She looked tired, Margot thought. She wore an apron over a limp brown dress that had definitely seen better days. Her grayish hair was beginning to tumble out of its hairpins. "How was the journey? Not too tiring?"

"Not a bit." Margot tried to be pleased to see her, but she could already feel the familiar tensing in her stomach. There was no use denying it; she was jealous of her mother.

"Where's James?" she said.

"Upstairs. He's just woken up from his nap. Shall we go and say hullo?"

"If it wouldn't be too much trouble," said Margot stiffly. She felt obscurely criticized, as she often did at home, though the rational part of her mind could see that she had no reason to. She was also annoyed that James wasn't downstairs to meet her. All week, she had been counting the hours and then the minutes until she saw him. Was he being deliberately kept out of her way? No, surely not. She could feel the nerves buzzing in her arms and stomach. She must remember not to assume the worst of everybody.

James was sitting at his little table by the nursery fire, a plate of bread and milk and stewed plums in front of him. Margot's heart gave a leap. He was pushing a wooden horse across the table and humming to himself—a small, solemn-looking boy of two, with fair hair falling into his eyes, looking very much as she'd done as a child. The nursemaid, Doris, was sitting with her feet up on the nursery fender, reading what looked like a penny novelette. She started when they came in and thrust the book hastily to one side.

Margot's mother said, "Perhaps not on duty, Doris, do you think?" and Doris said, "No, ma'am, sorry, ma'am," confusedly.

James looked up as they came in and flushed pink with pleasure. "Mummy!" he said—not to Margot, of course, but to her mother. He pushed aside the chair and ran over to her. Margot's mother picked him up.

"Hullo, darling. Look who's here!"

At this, James went suddenly shy and whispered, "Ernest 'n' Margot."

"Aren't you going to say hullo?" said Doris, and he buried his head in Margot's mother's shoulder.

Margot scowled. She was hurt by James's shyness and

hurt that he hadn't seemed pleased to see her. The glimpse of Doris with the novelette alarmed her too. She'd never been sure about Doris, who was sixteen and the daughter of one of the local farmhands. Should Mother have hired someone so young? Of course, their own nanny was too poorly now with rheumatics and had gone to live with her married daughter, and Margot knew servants were hard to find, but still—couldn't Mother have found someone more suitable now that the War was over and everyone was coming out of the services?

And then there was James himself. He looked so much older! How was it possible that a child could change so much in a few short months? What sort of mother was she, to stay away from him for so long?

She cleared her throat and said, "Hullo, James."

James wriggled and buried his head further into her mother's collarbone.

Ernest fumbled in his pocket. "I bought you a present, Jamie-o."

James's head lifted in interest. Margot felt another squirm of jealousy—why hadn't she thought of that?

"Look, James—see what your brother's bought you," said Doris.

Margot felt a flash of hatred.

Ernest brought out a piece of barley sugar on a string,

somewhat covered in pocket fluff and what looked like biscuit crumbs.

Margot's mother said, "Really, Ernest!"

"Look, it's a sweetie!" Doris said. Then, as James still tended to shyness, "Go on, then, pet—you take it."

James ventured far enough out to grab the string and retreated again.

Doris, clearly trying to make up for the novelette, asked, "What do you say?" and he mumbled, "Tank you," into the barley sugar.

With a glance at Margot, her mother said, "He'll soon open up. Shall we ring for tea?"

"I don't mind," said Margot. "Whatever you'd rather."

She was determined not to show that she cared.

LATER

• •••◦►)◄◦••• •

AFTER NURSERY TEA, MARGOT WAS SENT UPSTAIRS—
as she always was as a child—to rest before it was time to
dress for dinner. She was to sleep in her old bedroom, the
one she had shared with Jocelyn and was now Jocelyn's
own. Once upon a time—was it really only three years
ago?—her side of the room had been a mess of stockings,
powder compacts, toast crumbs, and illustrated weeklies.
Now her bed stood neatly made and impersonal. Jocelyn's
possessions had colonized what had been Margot's territory: her books on the shelves, her clothes in the drawers,
her old rag dolls lounging on the windowsill next to Margot's ballerina music box and the potbellied piggy bank
that said A PRESENT FROM SCARBOROUGH across its back.
As always when she came home, Margot was oddly pleased

to see that her influence was still present. There was only so much one could take to a cubicle in a boardinghouse. In the drawers of the dressing table, there were old hair grips and scrapbooks, pressed flowers from dances, and half-empty bottles of perfume. Old clothes still lay folded in her chest of drawers. There was even—somewhere—a lock of James's hair and his first little outfit, hidden away with old diaries and love letters from Harry, letters she couldn't bear to take with her to Durham.

Harry.

She would have to reply to him. Otherwise she would turn up at church on Christmas Day and there he would *be*.

She sat down on the bed. Jocelyn, who had come up behind her with the other case, said, "I think it's going to be rather a strange Christmas this year. Our first real one since the War—with everyone here, I mean."

"Has Mummy been completely sick-making about it?" Margot said. "Stephen home and all that?"

Last Christmas, Stephen had still been in Belgium, awaiting his discharge. James had been a cross, fretful child who screamed when held by anyone except Mother or Doris. And there'd been the influenza, their father so busy rushing around visiting the sick, comforting the bereaved. It had been a rather awful sort of Christmas all round.

And then Cecil Carmichael at the Willows had put a bullet through his brain. Nobody knew exactly why.

There'd still been food shortages, everything so expensive, none of the boys home yet, and a sort of dull, miserable exhaustion. It had been a bitterly cold Christmas, five inches of snow and frozen pipes, which later burst. The boardinghouse was cold too, of course, but there was nothing quite like the cold of home. Vicarages, Margot's mother said, had a particular sort of cold to them: big, drafty old rooms, high ceilings, too many bedrooms, threadbare carpets, and never enough money to light the fires.

This Christmas . . .

"When's Stephen coming?" she asked. "Do you know?"

"Not till the twenty-third," Jocelyn said.

"Does he still write to you? He doesn't to me."

Jocelyn shook her head. "Mummy hears from him now and then, I think. Not as often as she'd like."

Margot didn't reply. She was fond of her brother. She didn't like to think that he was unhappy.

Jocelyn, watching her, said, "Harry's home for Christmas."

"I know," said Margot. "He wrote to me."

"Oh!" Jocelyn's surprise was comical. "Are you two writing? I thought . . ."

"No," said Margot carefully. "His mother cabled me in February when they found out he was alive, and then she wrote me a long letter when he got back to England. And he wrote when he got out of the hospital. But I didn't write back. And then he sent me a letter saying he was going to be here for Christmas and shouldn't we talk.

"And what did you say?"

"I didn't. I haven't replied. I know! *I know!* But what could I say? *How* could I tell him about—about James—in a *letter?* Harry nearly died. He had pneumonia and exhaustion and heaven knows what else. His *mother* was probably reading his letters to him."

"But after he got out . . ."

Margot was quiet. Then, "I didn't know how to," she said. "I couldn't bear it if he . . . if . . ."

"But James is . . . well, he's as much Harry's child as yours, isn't he?" said Jocelyn.

"I know," she said. "But nobody thinks like that, do they? The girl is the one whose honor is defiled or whatever rot they spout. The boy is just being a boy. Father's practically a saint, and if even he doesn't think like that, I don't very well see how Harry is supposed to."

She stood up abruptly, went across to her suitcase, and began pulling out clothes. "Gracious, this house is cold!" she said. "I'm going to put on another petticoat."

Jocelyn did not reply.

FATHER

---◆◆◆◆◆◆◆---

FATHER.

Margot's father was a small, mild-mannered man, his hair thinning, his eyes blinking behind wire-rimmed spectacles. He looked like the sort of clergyman who spent his days chasing butterflies or writing monographs on Roman coins. In fact, he was one of the hardest workers Margot had ever met.

His life was spent rushing from meeting to crisis to service to bedside. He was universally loved, by both the poor of his parish and the Churchy Ladies who called him *the poor dear vicar* and worried about how tired he looked. He had been rather a distant figure in Margot's early childhood—her two gods had been Nanny and Mother—but as she grew older, she'd begun to wonder if perhaps they might have been good friends, the two of them. Her father spoke a lot of sense sometimes. She had grown up not thinking very much about him, and now she was beginning to dimly feel what she had lost.

Because she *had* lost it. The business with James had buckled her family bonds out of shape entirely. Her mother wasn't just her mother anymore; she was now also the mother of Margot's son, and their every interaction was weighed down by that knowledge. And her father . . .

She avoided her father whenever possible.

In a house where all the laundry was sent out by her mother, it had been impossible to hide her condition for long. Margot's knowledge of the facts of life had come from Stephen and a boy called Tucker he'd brought home from school, and nobody had mentioned that bleeding had anything to do with it. After two missed bleeds, it was her mother who had confronted her with the possibility of a baby. Her mother who had taken her to the doctor— not a local doctor but a clinic in York. Her mother who had sat tight-lipped and furious through the consultation, then taken her back on the train and broken the news to Father.

Margot's memory of it was like vertigo, like a waking nightmare. *Oh no oh no oh no oh no.* Not this. Not now.

The look of shock on her father's face when he was told

the news was one she would carry with her to the grave. He had not looked like that when war was declared or when baby Charlotte had died. It was as though he had been attacked. As though the very bedrock of his family was crumbling. He had stared at her, and then he had said, "My God, Margaret. How could you be so stupid?"

"I—" Margot stammered. "I—I didn't think—"

"That much is evident," he'd said. He'd sat down, rubbed his hands over his face, and stared at her bleakly through his fingers.

"I'm sorry," she'd said, and he'd shaken his head.

"This is going to take some forgiving," her mother had said.

Margot could not remember making a decision about the baby and what to do about it. She had known, of course, that this could happen, but she had always assumed that Harry would be there. She had imagined cabling him the news and Harry rushing back to marry her. Harry would not let her face this alone.

But Harry was missing in action. He'd been gone for a month.

He was almost certainly dead.

"Perhaps we could both live here?" she had suggested rather feebly, and her parents' expressions had been a picture.

"I really don't think that would be best, dear," her mother had said. Then, "Don't you want a life for yourself? A husband, a family?"

And Margot had agreed that she did.

Oddly, nobody had suggested giving the baby up. Her father had worked with several orphanages in his long career and had said mildly, "Not an orphanage, I don't think," and Margot had agreed in relief.

It was only later, presumably after some private conversation between her parents, that Margot's mother had told her what the arrangement was to be. It had all turned out to be surprisingly easy to manage. Nobody had been very shocked when she left school. Since the telegram about Harry and the realization that she was in trouble, she had given up any pretense at schoolwork. Her weeping fits and absences had been treated at first with sympathy—she wasn't the first pupil to lose someone in the War—but her mother's announcement that Margot was going to Durham for a secretarial course and a new start had been greeted with undisguised relief.

Nor had anyone raised any questions when her mother made it discreetly known that she was expecting again and going to a maternity home for the last three months of her confinement. Her mother was in her forties, exhausted with the running of the household, and after what had happened with Charlotte . . . No, nobody was very surprised at this precaution.

Margot had kept her condition hidden until the beginning of the summer holidays. Then they had left—her mother to stay with an aunt, and she to the mother-and-baby home with other similar unfortunates.

She could not remember being asked her permission. She supposed she could have refused, but what would have been the alternative? The idea of supporting herself and a baby, alone, at seventeen, was impossible.

Her overwhelming feelings had been panic and shame, and the desperate, miserable sense of a nightmare from which she could not wake.

But somehow her father's reaction was one of the worst memories of all. After that, she had avoided the vicar when she could, and on occasions when they were in the same room, she spoke to him as little as possible. Her father was famous throughout the parish as a good Christian man. He forgave drunks and tramps and adulterers and the men who tried to steal the lead from the church roof.

But he couldn't forgive her.

THE IMPOSSIBILITY OF WRITING A SIMPLE LETTER

The Vicarage Church Lane Thwaite
North Yorkshire
19th December 1919

Dear Harry,
    Thank you for your letter. I am sorry I did not write before. I did not know what to say.

Margot stared at this for a while. Even to her it looked feeble. She screwed it up and threw it into the wastepaper basket. Then she dipped her pen into the inkpot and started again.

Dear Harry,

I would be very pleased to see you when you are home for Christmas. I was so pleased when I found out you weren't dead.

Now she sounded like an aunt congratulating him on passing the School Certificate. It didn't convey at all the mess she'd been in when the cable arrived. And two *pleaseds* was poor style.

She screwed up the letter and hurled it into the basket. Then she dipped her nib into the inkpot again.

Dear Harry,

She stopped. What did she want to say to him exactly? If she couldn't be honest . . .

She would have to say something.

I am so sorry. I have behaved unforgivably. I cannot tell you why in a letter.
I would be very glad to see you.

Was *glad* too indifferent? She remembered the love letters she had written to him as a sixteen-year-old and winced.

Please let me know when would be convenient.

Now she sounded as though she were arranging a visit from the sweep. But what else could she say? She *couldn't* gush.

She stared at the letter, then dipped her pen slowly in the inkpot for the last time.

                                        Yours

Yours what?

                                        Yours,
                                        Margot

There.

HARRY

——————— ···✦✖✦··· ———————

HARRY SINGER HAD ARRIVED IN MARGOT'S LIFE
with an explosion when she was fifteen years old.

His mother had moved to the village with her children
at the start of the summer—an exciting event at the best of
times. His father was a general practitioner who had been
forced out of retirement by the War and sent to a military
hospital. The family home had been shut up, and Harry's
mother had moved the children to Thwaite for the dura-
tion and never left.

Harry was a long, rangy boy in his late teens, with dark,
floppy hair and a perpetual look of one about to grow out
of whatever clothes he was put in. He wasn't exactly handsome, though he certainly wasn't ugly either. *Nice-looking*,
her mother said, and that was perhaps closer to it. He had

an *attractive* face. He was someone you could sit next to and be sure of having a good time. Someone who would talk about books, and make your little sister a daisy chain, and buy you an ice cream when you'd forgotten your purse, and even talk to the most awful of Father's Churchy Ladies and look like he was enjoying himself. There was something about him . . . a confidence. A happiness. He was happy, in himself and in his place in the world. To Margot, who knew very few young men beyond Stephen's awkward school friends and the boys from church, this was immediately appealing. Happiness. What a gift.

This was 1916, and the ranks of eligible young men around her were thinning. This was not so much due to the machine gun as to the recruiting sergeant: anyone fit for service over the age of eighteen had disappeared into a world of army camps and letters from the Front.

It had been love at first sight.

She'd been standing just inside the church door, helping her mother hand out the hymnbooks. And the new family had walked into the church.

Harry's mother, with a garish green hat and an expression of tight-lipped anxiety. His sister Mabel, a gangly fourteen-year-old in a hideous magenta frock. Pricilla—Prissy—a little thing of twelve, all in pale peach. And then . . .

Harry. Her Harry.

She remembered the easy expression on his face as he'd looked round the church. How he'd smiled, and how her friend Mary beside her had said "Oh!" so comically. And then—oh hallelujah!—he'd looked up.

And seen her.

She remembered a physical jolt as he looked at her. He hadn't quite staggered backward, but it wasn't far off. It was a bodily reaction—like the clown at the circus when he turns and sees the mess his fellows have made of the floor. It made her want to laugh out loud with happiness. That was how she remembered him. A simple bringer of joy.

Her father was shaking his mother's hand. The Churchy Ladies were twittering excitedly. Harry slipped behind Prissy and came up to her.

"Hullo," she'd said idiotically.

And he'd said, "Hullo."

And they'd both started to laugh.

A MORNING WALK

HOW STRANGE TO BE BACK HOME! THERE WERE lamb chops and tapioca pudding for dinner. Afterward, they all went and sat in the drawing room. Jocelyn curled up on the sofa by the fire with her knitting, and their mother sat beside her, writing Christmas cards and sighing, "Goodness, wouldn't I like to strangle whoever invented Christmas cards! They mustn't have been a vicar's wife, whoever they were."

Ruth and Ernest, thrilled to be together again after so long, sprawled out on the hearth rug, whispering secrets and giggling.

James was brought down for half an hour after dinner, dressed in a gray romper suit and his nicest green jersey. He cried "Mummy!" in delight when he saw Mother, and ran across to her. She lifted him onto her knee, and he buried his face in her neck with obvious pleasure.

Father said, "Now then, old man," and James allowed himself to be lifted up and tipped upside down, just as they all had as children.

"Have you been a good boy for Doris?" Father asked.

And James said, "Good boy! Good boy!"

Father turned him upright and kissed him. James laughed out loud.

He stayed with their parents for a good ten minutes, watching Ernest and Margot with wary eyes. Margot tried not to show that she minded, and after a little persuasion, he allowed her to read him *The Tale of Two Bad Mice* and Ernest to demonstrate his new yo-yo tricks. It was like this every time she saw him after an absence, Margot reminded herself. He would soon forget his shyness and they'd be friends again. But it didn't make it any easier.

Her bedroom was icy, and her dreams were restless, full of Harry Singer telling her she was a coward and a traitor and an unnatural mother, and James crying because he didn't want to be left with her. It was late when she woke, she could tell by the lightness of the room. Jocelyn was still sleeping in the other bed. From where she lay, she could hear Ruth and Ernest squabbling on the stairs, James shouting about something in the day nursery, and

Edith, the cook-general, singing "O Come, All Ye Faithful" as she mopped the hall.

Breakfast was still laid out in the dining room. Margot helped herself to a cup of cold tea and a plate of kedgeree and ate it with her father's newspaper crossword for company. She was rather good at crosswords. People thought if you were pretty that meant you weren't clever. People always thought of plain-looking Jocelyn as the "clever one" and Margot as the "pretty one" (or the "trying one"—so difficult for the dear vicar). But Margot had always been third or fourth in her form, which was about where Jocelyn usually ended up.

Breakfast over, she wandered off in search of her mother. She wasn't in the drawing room or—apparently—the kitchen. Had she gone out? No, there she was, in the garden.

They had started keeping chickens during the War, like everyone else. Margot was fourteen when war broke out. In those days, they'd had a cook, a maid, Nanny of course, and a man who came once a week to look after the garden. Now there was just Doris and Edith. Every time Margot saw her mother, she looked busier, more tired, and sort of worn thin and limp-raggish. Today she was kneeling on the grass, wearing a coat that must have been ten years old at least, mucking out the nest box. It was rather disconcerting.

"There you are!" Margot said. "I'm so sorry, I seem to have missed breakfast altogether."

"Oh, darling, don't worry about it. I know what it's like when you're young. Enjoy it while you can! I don't suppose you get much chance to sleep in your boardinghouse."

"I'll say." Margot watched her mother. "How is everything? James looked well last night."

"He's very well." Her mother carried on pulling out the old straw without looking up. "But you can see that yourself."

"I . . ." Margot stopped. She felt, once again, the frustration that there wasn't a *script* for this. She knew how one was supposed to behave toward brothers, sons, parents. But this?

Was she supposed to be a second mother to James? Or ignore him completely? Or treat him like a favorite brother?

She'd been so determined that James would never feel his difference, that he would feel as loved by her mother as the other children were. She had stayed away deliberately so as not to get in the way. But was that right?

James's birth certificate had her name on it, of course. Mother: Margaret Allen. And one day he would read it. Margot thought about that moment far more often than she liked to admit. What would he think when he saw her name? Was it better to tell? But one couldn't tell a two-year-old a thing like that. What *would* he think when he saw that name?

Surely he would hate it—knowing they had all lied to him, knowing that his parents weren't his parents?

But would he hate *her*? Would he understand that she hadn't had a choice, that she was trying to be unselfish, to give him the best life she possibly could? How would he feel if she persisted in behaving like a distant older sister toward him? Surely a child would expect his mother to behave like one? But how could her mother love him properly if Margot was there, getting in her way? She'd *had* to leave them to their own devices; surely that was obvious? But would it be obvious to James?

How could one behave with honor toward the child he was now, the adult he would be one day, *and* her parents? It was impossible.

Her mother, still bent over the nest box, cut into these thoughts.

"Harry's home for Christmas."

Margot stiffened. "I know," she said. "Jocelyn told me."

"His mother was asking after you. Said she'd written, but you didn't reply. She couldn't understand it, she said. Wanted to know if you were . . . spoken for . . . by someone else."

Heavens, how awful this conversation was! Margot

could feel herself curling up with embarrassment inside.

"I told her you were an adult now and I didn't have the first idea what you got up to in Durham, but that as far as I knew you were still unattached."

"That must have been excruciating for you," said Margot, studying the peeling paint on the top of the hen-house.

"Well, darling, it was rather." Something in her mother's voice made her look up. "It's never a good idea to leave people hanging, you know. His mother is one of our most regular churchgoers, and I'm sure she has no intention of leaving the parish—and we certainly don't, of course. It does make life difficult for your father, you know."

"Perhaps Father might like to discuss it with me him-self, if he's got a problem with how I behave," said Margot, more bitterly than she'd intended. But really! Her father was marvelous at handling the villagers' problems. How absurd that he should be so bad at dealing with his own.

"Your father—" her mother began.

"Is a wonderful man. I know! To everyone else. He never talks to me! Surely you must see that?"

Margot's mother sighed. "Your father works incredibly hard," she said. "Particularly at Christmas. Perhaps you could try talking to him yourself?"

Margot flushed. She was . . . well, not a child, but not

exactly an adult either. And her father was her father. The idea that *she* might mend this breach herself was a new thought, and not entirely a pleasant one.

She turned the conversation back to Harry. "What do you *want* me to do, Mother?" she said. "Exactly? You were so down on Harry when you found out about—about—"

"Goodness!" Now it was her mother's turn to be surprised. "You couldn't expect your father and me to be *pleased*, could you? After what he did to you?"

No, of course she couldn't.

"Naturally we were upset," her mother went on. "And really both of you should have known better! But darling— you can't leave him hanging like that. You have to finish it one way or another."

"You mean I should tell him about James?" The thought was alarming.

"Well, I wouldn't go quite that far." The secrecy around James wasn't just to protect her, she knew. Awkwardnesses with Mrs. Singer about the church flowers wasn't the only way Margot might "make life difficult" for her father. "Not unless you were planning on marrying him. But for the boy's sake, you ought to finish things properly."

Finish things properly . . . How bleak those words were. She couldn't . . . Surely she couldn't have thought there might still be a chance . . . that she and Harry might . . . ?

But perhaps she always had, somewhere inside her. She had never loved anybody the way she loved Harry.

Something of this must have shown on her face, because her mother's expression altered.

"Well, darling! That puts rather a different spin on things, doesn't it?"

"I didn't say . . ." Margot began.

"Of course not." Her mother studied her. "He's a nice boy, Margot. I always liked him. He's had rather a rough war of it, from what his mother said. Being a prisoner and so forth."

"You liked him? But you were so fearfully against us marrying, and then . . ."

"Well, naturally you were both far too young to even think of marriage. Goodness, Margot! You were fifteen when you got engaged—and rather a young fifteen, at that. And then to get you in trouble and disappear . . ."

"He was captured! It was hardly deliberate!"

"Really, darling! He was being posted to the Front Line. He must have realized it was a possibility that something might happen."

Margot scowled.

Her mother, noticing, said, "Anyway, things are different now."

"I suppose they are." What a lot of new things she had

to think about! "I don't even know if he still likes me," she said weakly.

Her mother gave her the sort of look Nanny used to give when you said you couldn't remember if you'd washed your face or didn't know who had pushed Jocelyn into the puddle.

"From the impression his mother gave me," she said, "that isn't something you need to be worried about at all."

Oh heavens! What was one supposed to say to that? She gawped at her mother, who laughed.

"Think about it. And while you're here, there's something else I wanted to talk to you about. I don't suppose you could help me out on Monday, could you? I'm supposed to be organizing the Christmas party for the Sunday school, and it's Doris's half day, and I don't see how I'm expected to organize the games and so forth and keep an eye on James at the same time. You needn't do much," she added, piling straw into the nest box. "Just show him what to do in the party games and make sure he doesn't get into mischief."

"Of course," said Margot. "I'd love to." She felt a rush of gratitude toward her mother. *She didn't have to do that.*

But back inside, she was at something of a loose end. A good daughter—Jocelyn, for example—would, she supposed, be offering to help her mother with all the hundreds of jobs that needed doing in a vicarage in the week before Christmas. And there were her own preparations to finish—gifts to wrap, Christmas cards to buy and post, local friends to see if she could bear to. Yet Margot didn't feel like doing any of them.

Harry would have gotten her letter by now. It would have come by the morning post. Perhaps he'd reply this morning. Maybe his letter would arrive this afternoon or in the evening post.

She shook herself. It had been sent. There was nothing she could do about it now.

Fired by this resolution, she went up to the nursery. It was evidently time for James's walk. Doris was wrestling him into a coat—James protesting, "No! I do it!"

"No, Master James." Doris grabbed his arm and thrust it into the sleeve. "We haven't got all day."

"Why can't he do it himself?" Margot spoke more sharply than she'd intended. But really! Manhandling a child like that!

Doris dropped his arm and gave her a look Margot couldn't identify.

"As you wish, miss."

James, released from her hold, wriggled himself around, trying to get his arm backward and into the other sleeve. Margot watched, trying not to intervene. She hadn't realized before quite how complicated putting on a coat was.

James was growing more and more frustrated. "I can't!"

"Here," Margot stepped forward, relieved. "Let me—"

"*No!* I do it!"

He wrenched his arm back again and dissolved into furious sobs.

"No help!"

Margot glanced at Doris. Her face was carefully neutral, but Margot was sure she could detect an *I told you so* lingering unspoken.

"Look—if you'd just let me . . ."

He was properly crying, his face flushed, tears streaming down his cheeks. Margot watched helplessly. She was used to children, of course, being one of five, but still . . . Ernest was eight now. She'd forgotten how quickly small children went from total composure to absolute despair.

Determinedly not meeting Doris's eye, she said, "*Can* he put his own coat on?"

"Not really, miss," said Doris. "It's just he's at that age when they want to do everything for themselves. There, Master James," she said comfortably, patting him on the back. "Your sister doesn't want to see you upset like that!"

Doris was behaving very well, Margot thought. She watched meekly as the nanny put James into his coat, helped him do up the buttons, and gave him his hat.

"Now, just you show your sister how well you can put your own hat on!" she said, and Margot made obedient admiring noises.

"We were just going for our walk," said Doris when this was finished. If she was wondering what Margot was doing in her nursery, she didn't show it. "We're going to feed the duckies, aren't we, pet?"

"Would you like me to take him?" Margot said. "I'd love to, honestly. And I expect you've got things to be getting on with here, haven't you?"

The breakfast things were still spread over the nursery table. Margot winced. She hadn't meant to sound as though she were criticizing her.

But Doris just said, "That would be very nice, wouldn't it, Master James? Would you like to go for a walk with your sister?"

"We going feed the ducks," James said. His disinterest in her was obvious. Margot tried not to show that she cared.

OUTSIDE, THE AIR WAS ICY. THE LITTLE VILLAGE looked just as it always did—gray stone houses and laborers' cottages clustered around the green and the duck pond. Smoke was rising from the chimneys, and the grass and roads were stiff with frost. Here and there, Model Ts had begun to appear in front of the houses. But otherwise it could have been any wintry afternoon from her childhood.

Margot walked down the gravel road to the green, holding James's hand, thinking back to how she and Stephen and Jocelyn had taken this walk with Nanny, paper bags full of stale bread clutched in their mittened hands. She couldn't remember being quite as young as James, but she could remember the agonies of being five or six—the awfulness of not being allowed a beautiful ringleted doll like the one Betty Helcroft owned, the agony of being smaller than Stephen and of Nanny taking Jocelyn's side in battles. *Don't be so naughty to your little sister! A big girl like you should know better!*

Had she been awful? She supposed she had. She remembered her frustration that Jocelyn was always thought clever and Stephen brave, and she was . . . what? Pretty. And difficult.

Once upon a time, she had been difficult.

But James seemed happy enough. He'd forgotten his shyness, trotting along beside her, his hair extravagantly blond, just like her own.

"Come on, Jamie-o," she said.

He'd stopped by the Warners' hedge. "What dat, Margot?"

"That—it's holly berries. They come out at Christmas. They'll be decorating Daddy's church with it."

"Want."

"Oh—no, Jamie-o, it belongs to the Warners. You can't just pick other people's plants, it's not allowed. Come on."

She tugged on his hand. His face dissolved and he began to cry. Margot watched him helplessly. They'd barely spent fifteen minutes together and she'd made him cry twice.

"All right," she said quickly. "All right, I'm sorry! Please don't cry, darling. Here you go."

She reached up and plucked a holly twig off the bush, taking care to choose a piece with berries on. James's tears miraculously vanished, and he held up his hands for it.

"Careful—it's prickly."

"Prickly."

"Yes—it's got prickles, look."

She showed him, testing her finger against the prickles. "See—ow!"

He laughed and did the same. "Ow!"

"Yes, but do really be careful, darling; you could hurt yourself. Look—where do you want it? On your hat? In your buttonhole?"

They tried the holly twig in various places before settling on James's buttonhole.

"Beautiful!" she said, and he beamed at her before trotting off down the road toward the duck pond. He *did* like being with her.

They crunched their way across the frozen grass. "Look, James, that's called frost—you see, where the grass is all white?"

At the pond on the common, they threw their crusts to the ducks, who gobbled them with satisfactory enthusiasm.

"More!" said James.

Margot said, "All gone!" and held out her hands.

James giggled and copied her. "All gone!"

It seemed a shame just to go back home.

"Shall we go and get some sweets at the shop?" she suggested, and James agreed enthusiastically.

But this turned out to be a bad idea. The village shop was farther away than she'd remembered—or rather, it was where it always had been, at the other end of the village, next to the school, but she hadn't realized how long it would take a two-year-old to walk three-quarters of a mile. James seemed to want to stop at every doorway, to pick up every stick, and to investigate every stone in the road. He wanted to drag his hands along every wall and jump in every puddle.

Margot could feel her patience draining away. "Look, Jamie-o," she said encouragingly. "There's the shop—look! Don't you want some sweeties? We could get some Liquorice Allsorts—or some Dairy Milk. Come on—I'll race you."

This worked, and they spent a happy ten minutes in

the grocer's, deciding between the various sweets available, until James settled on a bag of Liquorice Allsorts (he loved liquorice, just as she had as a child). Margot also bought some cocoa powder for the nursery—she knew Doris loved it—and some Christmas cards (she supposed she ought to send them). On an impulse, she also bought chocolate for Ernest and Ruth (their Christmas presents were rather paltry this year—most of her money had been spent on James). And then, feeling rather guilty for the way she'd treated her mother, she bought a potted fern and a packet of biscuits as a peace offering.

They made several parcels when the grocer had finished wrapping them. Margot let James sit on the wall outside the grocer's and eat his Allsorts, feeling rather rebellious (Nanny had never let them eat in public). Then they headed back home.

It was now that the trouble started. At first, James began to lag. Margot tried not to be impatient, but it was hard— she was beginning to get cold, and the vicarage was on the other side of the village.

"Come on, Jamie-o," she said. "Home time!"

James dropped to his knees. "Carry me!"

"I can't, darling." She felt a flutter of panic. "I've got my hands full—I can't carry the parcels *and* you. Look, it's not that far."

But to a two-year-old it apparently was. With much cajoling on her behalf and whining on James's, they made it to the edge of the village green, where he refused to go any farther.

"James, please," she said. "You made it all the way here! We're nearly there."

But James had reached the end of his endurance. He began to cry. She bent down to embrace him, but he pushed her away.

"No! Want Doris! Want Mummy!"

"Please, James," she said again. "It's not far—come on . . ." But James sank to his knees again and began to howl—mouth open, cheeks red, tears streaming down his face.

Margot considered her options. She could carry James if she didn't have the shopping—would he be all right here on his own if she went back to the village shop and left the parcels there to be picked up later? She glanced back down the street. It was a good five minutes there and five minutes back, not to mention however long it would take to explain to the grocer. Even supposing she could run, which she couldn't. The gravel road through the village would, she supposed, eventually be tarred over if everyone carried on buying motorcars, but right now it was thick and claggy and potholed, with two deep ruts where the cart tracks ran. You couldn't run along it—not easily—and certainly not in petticoats.

Could she leave the parcels here and come back for them? A spatter of rain against her cheek suggested not. She looked up at the sky. Gray, heavy clouds as far as she could see. She thought of the Christmas cards and chocolates in the brown-paper parcels. They would be ruined. And she had no money left for more. She glanced around, looking for help, but the street was silent. Her father would be on good terms with every family in the village—or so it seemed—but Margot didn't have his confidence. The houses here were smaller, laborers' cottages, and the thought of knocking and asking for help was impossible—she would rather abandon the Christmas presents than do that. But perhaps . . . At the top of the next street was Miss Dawson's house. Miss Dawson was one of her father's Churchy Ladies, a particular favorite of Margot's. She could remember being given comfits when out delivering the parish magazine with her father. Miss Dawson would look after the parcels—and if she were out, they could be left on her porch at least. Then Margot could carry James home. Two streets—James could walk two streets, couldn't he?

She crouched down beside him in the dirt.

"James, listen," she said. In desperation she threw the

precepts of her childhood to one side. "Would you like another sweetie?"

He couldn't stop crying, but he gave a half-nod, shuddering.

"All right, well—we're going to walk to a lady's house, Miss Dawson." (Would he know who Miss Dawson was?) "It's not far, and when we get there, you can have a sweetie. And then Margot will carry you . . . Oh no, James, please don't cry . . ."

"Carry me!"

It was hopeless. She hauled him up by the armpits, and he collapsed himself, stiffening his back, slackening his muscles so she had to take the whole of his weight.

"Come on, James. James, *please* . . ."

"Excuse me?"

She looked up and felt the blood rush into her face.

Because of course it was him. Of course, *of course* it was. Like something in a penny novelette.

Harry Singer, all dark hair and army greatcoat, with a scarf in bright scarlet wrapped casually around his neck. He was broader than she'd remembered, and taller and older too, much older than he had a right to be after three years apart. But still nice-looking. Still with that some-thing—was it kindness?—hovering in his eyes. Oh God. And she must look older too. Sometimes, when she saw herself in the mirror, she felt a hundred years old. Of all the times to see him! Kneeling there in the dirt, her skirts splashed with mud, James howling and thrashing in her arms.

Had he gotten her letter yet? If not—how awful!—what must he think of her? She scrambled to her feet, red-faced.

Hullo, Harry. This is your son. She had a helpless urge to giggle.

"It's my fault he's crying," she said desperately. *He's nice, really, honor bright. He's only behaving like this because I don't know how to look after him properly. Oh God, he'll never want us now.* "I made him walk to the shop, and now he won't walk back. He wants to be carried, but I've got these parcels . . ."

"Most unfortunate," said Harry solemnly. "Perhaps you might permit me to assist?"

He talked like a gentleman in a novelette too. She'd forgotten he had this habit when nervous. It came from his father, who really did talk like this, and wrote articles for journals about the deplorable state of diets for urban children just like this too. Somehow, knowing Harry was nervous calmed her down. It made her feel protective, the way it always used to, back when they were both children and love was simple.

She was smiling despite herself. Ridiculous to be won over so easily by a man! And yet . . . at that moment, she would probably have accepted a marriage proposal from anyone who offered to help.

"Thank you," she said. Then, "Look, Jamie! This gentleman is going to help Margot carry her parcels, so she can carry you!"

James didn't seem to have heard her.

Harry crouched in the mud beside him. "Would you like to be carried home?" he asked solemnly.

He had his own little sisters, she remembered. And how prosaic this first meeting between father and son! Because it was simultaneously like something out of a novelette and also immensely ordinary. The gray Yorkshire drizzle, the wet parcels, the crying child. For so long after that *missing in action* telegram, she had wondered if he would ever come back. How awful if he never met his son! How wonderful if he were alive, how wonderful to be able to introduce him to James, to have somebody to share this joy and this grief.

But it wasn't like that at all. And the words wouldn't come.

James stared, the closeness of a stranger enough to stop his tears. He retreated backward into Margot's legs and buried his face in her side. She put her arm around him, realizing that she ought to have been trying to comfort him before.

"All right, darling," she said. And then, to Harry, "If you really wouldn't mind . . ."

He took the brown paper parcels into his arms. There was another spot of rain, and then another, and then suddenly it was raining properly—not heavily, but enough to make James whimper.

"All right," she said again, and lifted him onto her hip.

He was heavier than she'd expected, and an awkward weight against her breastbone. Still, there was nothing else for it. Not looking at Harry, she set off back toward the vicarage, Harry beside her.

They walked without talking. Margot couldn't stop herself from glancing at him. He looked like a different person! His hair was darker than she remembered, and thicker, and it fell in a tumble over his eyes. And his smile! She'd often wondered if he'd lost that easy happiness after two years as a prisoner of war, and looking at him now, she had her answer. The ease had gone—his happiness was not a straightforward thing, and he knew that now. But the delight in the world was still there. He had fought whatever demons one found in prisoner-of-war camps, and he had won. The weight of the sky may have wobbled on his shoulders, but now he carried it securely again.

She envied him, as she always had. Her own sky had

fallen onto her head, and she hadn't the first notion how to lift it up again.

She looked at him, almost against her will, to see if his eyes were still the same color, and caught him looking at her. She flushed and he laughed.

"I'm sorry," he said. "I didn't mean to discomfort you."

"No, I'm sorry." She dared her eyes to remain on his face. His expression was friendly, but there was a wariness there too, something kept back. She swallowed. "It's good to see you. And I really am very grateful . . ."

"My pleasure." He bowed his head. Then, "It's good to see you too."

She blushed. Were they—surely he couldn't expect to have the whole conversation now? He couldn't—not with James there? Could he?

"Are you—I was sorry to hear you were ill. I hope you're quite recovered?"

Now she was doing it too! Any moment now he would ask why she hadn't written, and she wouldn't know what to say and it would be awful. Couldn't they just talk about the weather like normal repressed Englishmen?

"Oh yes, quite."

A small pause. They were at the edge of the green. "And who's this? A new brother?"

So he definitely didn't know. She wasn't sure how

well-kept a secret it was, if at all. Her parents knew, of course, and her friend Mary, and Jos and Stephen. But what about the servants? Had her parents told any of their friends? Surely, *surely* they must have done?

Sometimes Margot thought that nobody knew—other times that half the village was maintaining a polite fiction of ignorance. Was this a test? But Harry's face betrayed nothing but mild interest.

He's your son.

She opened her mouth, but the words wouldn't come. She stared at him, gaping, then said, all in a rush, "Oh—yes—I mean. This is James. He's—yes. James."

"Hullo, James."

He'd always been good with small children; better than she was, really. Ruth and Ernest had adored him.

She should just tell him.

"And you?" he said politely. "Are you keeping well?"

No, they were just going to talk as though they were in a drawing room.

"Oh! Very well, thank you. I'm a typist now, if you can believe that."

He made a polite noise that began as agreement, then reversed as he realized his mistake, and ended as a sort of amused confusion.

"Mmm . . . aaahhmm . . . Mh."

She giggled. He flashed her a sudden, wonderful smile, bright as poppies in a cornfield.

"I'm sorry," he said. "I just . . . It's good to see you."

"You already said that."

"Well. Well, so it is."

They were turning onto the road that led to the vicarage. She could see curious eyes watching them from the front garden. Ruth and Ernest, halfway up the apple tree. Curse them! What were they doing outside in this rain? She slowed, instinctively trying to prolong the walk. If only she hadn't hurried so at the beginning! Except . . . with Ruth's frankly curious gaze upon her, she found she could think of nothing to say. At least . . . nothing she could say with those awful infants ogling her from among the branches.

Damn him! Damn them!

"It's awful, really," she said quickly, desperate to say something that was real at least, something that didn't belong in a drawing room. "I work in a foul school full of dreadful girls. I abhor it."

They were at the gate. Ruth and Ernest came sliding down the tree and surged toward them like puppies.

"Harry!"

"Harry Singer!"

"What are you doing here?"

"Are you coming in?"

"Goodness, it's wet!"

"Do come in—we're about to have luncheon."

"*Do* come, Harry, and tell us all about being a captive."

"Was it ghastly?"

She could strangle them.

James was tugging on her sleeve. "Too wet, Margot. Too wet!"

Harry was detaching himself from Ruth and Ernest with apologies and gifts of sixpences and an armful of brown-paper parcels each. James was wriggling out of her arms, his furious little head shaking hair into her eyes. Her mother appeared at the doorway, and his face collapsed again, into that perfect, mouth-open picture of infant grief. Margot's mother scooped him up and *shh*ed him, the expression on her face at comical odds with the gentle motion of her hands.

"There you are! Goodness, Margot, I thought you'd kidnapped him! Where on earth did you go? I sent Ruth and Ernest down to the duck pond; they said you were nowhere in sight."

"We just—I just—and then . . ."

She turned to Harry, hoping to salvage something of the situation.

But he was gone.

GLORY DAYS

———·•··◆··•·———

"MUMMY! MARGOT AND HARRY WERE TALKING, and she won't tell us what he said!"

The children burst into luncheon with more than their usual energy. Really, how did Mother cope with them?

"He didn't say anything beyond the usual pleasantries," said Margot stiffly. "And you two should keep your noses out of other people's business."

"I'm going to be a lady detective when I grow up," said Ruth. "So I *have* to put my nose in people's business. Are you still engaged? Are you going to get married? Oh goody, cottage pie! My favorite! Didn't he look dashing? Don't you think he's dashing, Margot?"

"I think little girls should eat their luncheon and stop talking such nonsense," said their mother.

Ruth looked indignant. "It isn't—"

"And I've got some news that will interest you big girls," their mother continued. "The Hendersons are having a ball at New Year."

Immediate, rapturous attention from Ruth. Pleasant surprise, despite herself, from Margot, and an expression of vague horror from Jocelyn. Only Ernest continued chewing his green beans with an air of indifference. (James was eating upstairs with Doris.) The Hendersons lived in the big house in the village. They were nominally part of her father's parish, though in practice they appeared in church only on feast days. The vicar sat on several local committees with Mr. Henderson, and Basil Henderson had been married in his church, in a great rush, two weeks before the Battle of the Somme. "Their first ball since the War. I expect you older children will be invited."

"Heavens," said Margot. "What on earth will we wear?"

Clothes were always a problem in the vicarage. Their father might be a gentleman, and expected to send his sons to public school, but he earned comparatively little. Margot and her sisters had spent their childhoods in hand-me-downs from various relations and party dresses made of their mother's cut-down ball gowns. Their mother was the youngest daughter of a country squire and had led what always seemed like a wonderfully glamorous late-Victorian adolescence, attending hunt balls and country house parties, before settling tamely for their father and a drafty vicarage, and a life of missionary teas and Sunday school catechisms and leaking oil stoves and rising damp.

She studied Margot now with cool appraisal. "You *might* fit into my blue taffeta. It would be worth a try. I expect Jocelyn will get away with your old gray velvet; she's just about young enough to pull it off."

"Me?" said Jocelyn. "*I'm* invited?"

"I believe so," said her father. "Matthew Henderson said *Stephen and your girls*, though I don't think he was talking about Ruth. I expect you'll get a proper invitation card soon enough."

"I say," said Jocelyn. "Does this mean I'm *out*?"

Already, *coming out* was becoming an old-fashioned concept—how much had changed since the War!—but Margot supposed people still did it. Of course, as a vicar's daughter, Jocelyn wouldn't have a coming-out ball like Marjorie Henderson had had. But it was still an occasion, one's first grown-up ball as a young lady.

Her mother's face fell.

"Oh Lord," she said. Then, seeing Jocelyn's expression, "Oh, Jos, I'm sorry. It's just—well—if you're coming out, I suppose the gray velvet really *won't* do, and you'll need proper shoes and—heavens, why can't little girls stay children forever?"

Margot looked at Jocelyn, whose face was a picture of horror. Swallowing, she said, "Jocelyn can have the blue taffeta if she wants."

"But what will *you* wear?" said Jocelyn.

The blue taffeta was beautiful, supposing it fitted. But Jocelyn should have something nice for her first ball.

"I expect I've got something from my prewar days," Margot said, trying to remember her adolescent wardrobe. "The red, perhaps?"

Her mother said briskly, "I'm afraid the moths have rather gotten into the bodice. I wonder—shall we have a look in Glory Days?"

Glory Days was the chest where their mother kept her old ball gowns and cloaks, the children's outgrown party dresses, and bits and pieces of material for rainy days. When Margot had been a child, Glory Days had always been like something out of a fairy tale.

"There surely can't be anything left in Glory Days now, can there?" Margot said doubtfully.

"Well—when Granny died, there were some things we inherited," her mother said. "Nothing you could wear as it is, but perhaps we could alter them . . ."

Opening Glory Days was an event in itself. The chest

lived on the landing that led to the servants' quarters; after luncheon, they all trooped upstairs to watch. Their mother opened the lid with great solemnity. Every dress and wrap had to be lifted out and considered, and everything had a story, which had to be told. Most were family legends.

"That's the dress you and Nanny made me for Peggy Burrows's tenth birthday—do you remember?"

"I certainly do! And you spilled lemonade all down the front of it, and I could have spanked you there and then—the trouble Nanny and I took over it."

"Look! There's the dress you wore to the dance where you met Daddy."

"So it is." Their mother looked at it fondly. "Heaven knows what I was thinking. I'm surprised your father looked twice at me."

"But he danced six dances with you and came round to call the next day. And Granny was horrified because he was only a poor curate, but you loved him anyway." The children knew the story by heart.

"Is this one of Granny's dresses?" It was black crepe de chine, very long and fussy. Ruth dragged it out of Glory Days, staring. "Goodness! It's ugly!"

"Granny had that made when Queen Victoria died.

Everyone wore black. You and Stephen had little black skirts, Margot, and black bonnets. Your father's church warden had eleven children, and he said to me, 'Ma'am, I'm very sorry the queen has died, but if she had to do it, I do wish it wasn't just after Christmas when money is so tight.' Poor fellow! He wasn't the only one who thought that, I'll be bound."

"There's a cloak as well." Margot held it up. It was black velvet, gloriously soft, and remarkably undamaged by moths. "Couldn't we do something with this? Just something simple."

"You always did look well in black, with that hair." Their mother took the cloak and spread it out on the floor. She was a keen dressmaker. "It's lovely quality, and there's plenty of it. I couldn't do anything before Christmas, mind."

"Naturally. I could help, perhaps?"

"Well . . . if you could . . ." Margot's mother got up suddenly, holding the black cloak against her. "Why don't you have a look through my patterns and see if you can find anything you like? I dare say there'll be something in there that we can make up in time."

And for a moment, it was almost like being a girl again.

5 Watery Lane Thwaite
North Yorkshire
20th December 1919

Hullo!

So lovely to see you today. (I said that already, didn't I? Well it was.) And lovelier still to come home to your letter.

Please may I come around tomorrow afternoon? Would 2 o'clock suit?

Harry

The Vicarage Church Lane Thwaite
North Yorkshire
20th December 1919

Dear Harry,

It was very lovely to see you too. Many thanks again for all your help with James.

I'm afraid we're not allowed to receive visitors on a Sunday. And I have to help Mother with a party on Monday morning. Would Monday afternoon suit?

Yours,
Margot

5 Watery Lane Thwaite
North Yorkshire
20th December 1919

    Monday afternoon it is! Tell your mother to expect me at 2 o'clock sharp.

    I really am ever so pleased to see you again, you know.

Harry

CHURCHGOING

CHURCH ON SUNDAY: JAMES LOOKING AN ABSO-
lute doll in gray knickerbockers and a little gray jacket. He
was quite the sweetest child in the Sunday school. Ruth in
a hideous green dress Margot had worn herself as a child.
All the Churchy Ladies twittering around her, "So lovely
to see you back, dear. And so grown up! Your dear father
must be *so* proud."

Tight smiles back. A self-deprecating "Oh *well* . . ." and
a quick change of subject.

The old church was absolutely freezing. Ice on the
windows, and the congregation all in coats and hats and
scarves. The roof beams decked out with holly and ivy, and
the nativity laid out in front of the altar, the manger empty
and waiting for the Christ child. As a little girl, Margot had

always loved coming into church on Christmas morning and seeing the baby in the manger. That was the moment when Christmas really began.

No Harry—he was a confirmed atheist, she knew, though he always used to come to the Christmas services—but his mother was there with the younger children. She was rather cold but very polite when Margot's mother insisted they say hullo. (*How* had her mother managed to stay on speaking terms with them all this time? English manners were incredible.) Yes, Harry was well and home for Christmas. Yes, he was going to study agriculture. (Agriculture?) He'd worked on a farm in Germany and gotten the taste for it. His uncle had a dairy farm near York, so it was in the family. (Actually, she could picture Harry as a farmer. He was a hard worker, and he loved the outdoors. He'd be miserable cooped up inside.) Yes, it had been a worry, he'd had pneumonia very badly, but he was much better now. He'd had a hard time of it this past year. (This with a meaningful look at Margot.)

Damn these people! Damn polite society! It wasn't as though she were even a Christian herself, really. She only came to church for her parents' sake.

There was dear Mary, with George and the children.

Her oldest friend.

"Darling!"

"Hullo, darling. Goodness, hasn't the baby grown!"

"They do that," said Mary, comfortable, happy Mary. Margot couldn't get used to her as a wife and mother. She was only twenty-two. Margot still thought of her as her pig-tailed friend from Sunday school days, sharing whispers and toffees behind their prayer books. "She's quite the pig, aren't you, angel? How long are you home for? You must come and see us."

"Oh, the whole holidays. I'd love to."

They arranged a date. Darling Mary. Margot had almost forgotten what it was like to have a proper friend like that.

1916

———◆————⟫⟪⟨————◆———

THAT SUMMER—THE SUMMER MARGOT TURNED
sixteen—had been like something out of a storybook.

Harry was going to be nineteen that September, and then
he was going to join up. He'd had a bad case of bronchitis
the year before and so had been exempt from conscription,
but he thought he'd pass the medical in September.

"I'd feel such a wart if I did anything else," he'd said.

Margot had thought he was probably right, but the idea
of it terrified her. Not that she'd ever really believed that
anything would happen to him. She'd been more con-
cerned about them being apart for months and months on
end. "How can I bear it?" she'd said to him.

"I don't suppose you will," he'd said cheerfully, "But
that's what women have to do in wartime, isn't it? Buck up!"

He'd agreed to wait until his birthday, so they had the summer at least.

"One summer!" she'd said, knowing as she did so that she was putting it on for dramatic effect, and he'd laughed and kissed her.

They'd belonged to each other from the moment they'd met. Perhaps she'd been deluding herself—could it really have been love? Was such a thing possible when you were fifteen and as much of an ass as she had been? Surely he must have been a bit of an ass too, an eighteen-year-old dragged to a village in the middle of nowhere, full of restless energy and frustration. What had he really seen in her? The recklessness? The adoration? The blond hair?

They'd both been bored silly, she remembered. Aside from a week in Scarborough, she'd been home all summer with—it seemed—nothing to do besides chores and music practice and dull church groups.

The previous summers, Margot had been willing enough to play about with Jocelyn and Stephen in the vicarage garden and on the common, going on excursions with Mother, on woodland picnics and walks on the fells, and day trips to Robin Hood's Bay. They'd helped their father with the Sunday school picnic and the church fête, dug halfheartedly in the flower beds, helped more enthusiastically with the fruit picking, made summer puddings and apple cakes, and spent long lazy afternoons reading in the vicarage garden.

In 1916, however, something had changed. Stephen was moody and frustrated, realizing, perhaps, that next year he would be eighteen and expected to fight. He seemed suddenly aware of his status as a young man, and he'd showed little interest in childish games. Margot too could feel herself becoming too old for childhood. She had spent a lot of the early part of the year locked in her bedroom, staring at her reflection in the looking glass and worrying about the life that lay before her. Would she ever find a husband? Why had no one fallen in love with her yet? She was fifteen, after all. Surely someone should have by now?

And then Harry Singer had walked into the church.

How frustrating their courtship had been! They could never be alone together. When he called at her house, her mother always insisted on waiting in the drawing room with them; when she called at his, one of his little sisters was forced to chaperone them, protesting loudly at the duty.

"Why can't you get engaged?" his sister Prissy had complained. "Then I won't have to sit here for hours watching you canoodle."

"Could we, though?" Margot had whispered while Prissy retreated behind her novel, sighing ostentatiously.

"Get engaged? Of course. But—"

"But what?"

"Well—will it really make any difference? Will your parents let us be alone together? Because I'm damn sure mine won't."

"Of course they will!" said Margot.

But they hadn't. Her parents had treated her engagement with something like amusement.

"Well, well, we'll see," her mother had said. And, "I hope you aren't expecting to get married before he joins up, are you?"

"Why shouldn't I?" Margot had retorted. She would be sixteen in July. But of course she had no intention of doing anything of the sort—how could she possibly get married? She was still at school. Nobody could expect her to run her own house—she was, for all reasonable purposes, a child. But to have the whole thing treated as a joke made her almost want to do it—just to *show* them.

As to being allowed to spend time on their own . . . "I think not, my dear," her father had said, and Jocelyn or her mother would be dispatched to sit in the drawing room whenever Harry appeared.

"Polite conversation!" said Harry as they said goodbye at the garden gate. He was an active young man, and sitting in the drawing room bored him senseless. He leaned in toward her. "What do you think would happen if I kissed you on the lips?"

Margot giggled.

"Goodness!" she'd whispered back. "I can't imagine. I rather think my mother might turn into a pillar of salt."

"Shocking behavior," he'd agreed, and he dropped a folded piece of paper into her hand.

She'd waited until he was gone and unfolded it.

2 o'clock. Make some excuse and meet me at the Harcourts' house?

And so it began.

THE HARCOURTS, A VILLAGE FAMILY, WERE AWAY for the summer. They had shut everything up and taken the servants with them, but before they left, they'd engaged Harry to water the plants, feed the cats, mow the lawns, and generally keep the garden in good order.

All that long summer, the Harcourts' house became their escape and their sanctuary. She would set off in the direction of Harry's, then—making sure nobody could see her—duck off into the lane down to the Harcourts'. Even now, remembering it, Margot felt the old shiver of excitement. The lane to the Harcourts' house was a pale green tunnel, the boughs of the trees meeting and intertwining over her head, the sunlight dappled through the leaves. To Margot, it felt like slipping through into a wild green kingdom, one where she and Harry were free to live as they chose.

And then, of course, there was the Harcourts' house itself. A modern white-brick bungalow with a half-wild garden ingeniously filled with grottoes and seats and bits of statuary. And at the end of the garden, the view over the valley, distant, smoky, and strangely beautiful. The empty house itself, the furniture covered with dust sheets, other people's crockery in the cupboards, and other people's books on the shelves. Other people's love letters, presumably, in the locked writing desks, and other people's nightdresses in the chest of drawers, although Harry—who was strictly honest about such things—would never look.

It had been such a strange and magical summer. They had spent every minute they could there, together. They had read the Harcourts' books, and made themselves little meals of corned beef and bread and butter, and brewed themselves tea on the Primus stove. Harry had done his chores around the garden, and she'd followed after him, picking the fruit and gorging on it—the sweetness of raspberries and apples, and gooseberries with sugar in the Harcourts' finest bone china bowls.

And whole afternoons in the Harcourts' guest bed.

The first time was her sixteenth birthday. Her best present had been a new summer frock in pale blue; her mother had sewn it, so she'd known it was coming, but it had been revealed in all its glory on her birthday morning.

Harry had cut a white rose from the garden and placed it in her hair.

"Sixteen today," he'd said.

"Now I'm really not a child anymore," she'd said, and he'd kissed her. She'd known what was coming as surely as he had; hadn't it been coming all that long, misty summer? She'd taken his hand and led him up toward the house.

Afterward, she often wondered how they could have been so reckless. She'd been young, but not a fool. She had a brother and older cousins, she knew the facts of life. She understood the risks they were taking. And Harry—surely Harry must have known how dangerous it was? Why hadn't it occurred to either of them to be more careful?

But it never had. To Margot, it had been all tied up with the magic of the Harcourts' house, its separateness from reality. The house had been like a place in a storybook, like Briar Rose's sleeping palace, like the Beast's rose garden. And as it happened, their luck had held. The summer had ended, and the Harcourts returned full of praise for the state of their garden. Harry had gone off to an army camp and sent her long, detailed love letters. She had gone back to school, and to the miserable realization that she was, in fact, still the child she always had been. In the sixth form, her engagement seemed an unreal thing, a summer game, a child's promise.

If James had happened that summer, there would have been time to do something about it. They might have been married before he went off to France. But James hadn't happened then.

He'd happened the last weekend Harry had leave, before he'd been sent to the Front. He'd sent a cable to the house—waiting until Friday, when her parents went to play bridge. She'd made up a story about a last-minute invitation to stay with her friend Peggy, who'd left school the year before. Then she'd caught the early train to his camp in Sheffield and they'd spent his last day of leave together.

The best bit had been the joy of seeing him on the station platform. He'd been standing there in his uniform, holding a single white rose, and beaming at her. She'd quite forgotten about looking sophisticated and ladylike, and had run into his arms. The feel of his chest against hers, the smile on his face . . . it had been perfect. A perfect moment.

But it hadn't lasted. The rest of the weekend was miserable. There was the gray, grimy city, full of men in uniform. Then he had to spend half their precious day together doing last-minute shopping for the trip to France. There was the worry about how much money the trip was costing, and the lingering sense that shouldn't it therefore be better? What was she doing wrong?

And then—oh horrors!—he'd pulled a cheap brass ring from his pocket.

"I thought you ought to wear it. For the—well, for the hotel, you know."

She'd burned with embarrassment. Pretending to be married so they could spend the night together! It was like something out of the worst sort of cheap novel, about as far away as one could get from the vicarage without actually becoming a chorus girl. What had seemed so magical and precious in the Harcourts' house suddenly felt dirty and shameful. It had spoiled the whole mood of the occasion.

The evening had gone wrong somehow too—she'd been stiff and cross, and he'd been a little drunk, and somehow nothing had quite worked the way it had in the Harcourts' house. They'd fought about nothing at all—though at the time it had seemed incredibly important—and then the next day he'd had to leave early to get back to the barracks, and she'd realized that she only had thruppence left to last her the whole way home. She'd bought three penny buns and eaten them slowly, but she'd forgotten about water and was so thirsty when she finally got back to the village that she nearly drank the water from the taps in the station lavatory. The whole thing was wretched and awful, and she wasn't sure who she was most angry with—Harry or herself or both. Maybe this was just what happened when things like war got in the way. Maybe this was what being nearly married to someone was like. Or maybe everything was over, and they'd never really been in love after all.

Two days later he'd left for the Front.

And then a month later the telegram. Missing in action.

It was the end of everything.

CHRISTMAS

·••·◦••∙◦»×«◦••∙◦••·

HOLY WEEK AND CHRISTMAS WERE THE BUSIEST times of year in the vicarage. The whole family had always been expected to pitch in and help. There were Christmas parties for the children at church, for the Girls' Friendly Society and the Mothers' Union, for the children whose parents came to the church soup kitchen, and for the old folk at the almshouses where Margot's father was chaplain. There was a carol service, a children's Christmas service, Midnight Mass, a special Christmas Day service attended by most of the village (up to and including the more pious of the guests at the big house), a Nativity play, and special Christmas services at the village school and the grammar school. On top of everything, there were Christmas cards to write to all the parishioners and Christmas presents to give and receive.

Margot's father got more Christmas presents than anyone she'd ever met. All of the Churchy Ladies gave him something, but so did heaps of unexpected people—women from the soup kitchen, poor families he'd helped with clothes or money, shut-ins he visited for Communion, all the many disconnected people whose lives he touched.

It was a rule in the Allen family that any presents received must be reciprocated. For years, Margot and Jocelyn and their mother had spent their evenings sewing simple presents for parishioners. Lavender bags and embroidered handkerchiefs and penwipers for the well-off. "Plain" sewing and knitting for the poor—"Can people *really* be grateful for a sock knitted by me?" Margot had famously once asked, aged ten.

Jocelyn, of course, was busy helping her mother with all the Sunday school affairs. Even Ruth was expected to help cut sandwiches and supervise games. And Stephen usually played the piano—he had always been a musical child, though he didn't have a piano in his digs in Sheffield, and as far as Margot knew he hadn't played at all since coming back from France.

There were two Christmas parties for the Sunday school children this year: one for children under ten, which included Ernest and James, and would be party games and a party tea; and one for children under fourteen, which included Ruth and would involve dancing—"Yuck!" said Ruth—and slightly more sophisticated fare.

The younger children's party was held on Monday in the church hall. Margot, Jocelyn, Ernest, and James went down early to help set out the food and bring across the props for the various games—the blindfold for blindman's bluff, the gramophone for the musical games, and the creased and battered vicarage donkey picture, a veteran of twenty years of pin the tail on the donkey.

When it came to it, however, Margot discovered that there was a limit to how helpful she could be while minding a two-year-old. She had come prepared with a ball and a train and a couple of picture books, but James showed no interest in playing quietly by himself while she buttered bread and laid out plates and glasses. He insisted on her full attention: "*Play*, Margot!" although this did not involve actual play so much as wandering around the church hall and the freezing garden, exploring every crack and cranny, stopping to investigate every stick and wall and plant and hole.

"What dat, Margot?"

"It's—um—it's a grating. It's—well, I'm not sure what it's for, exactly."

"Bird!"

"Yes, that's a bird. It's—a crow, I think. Or a rook, or

maybe a raven. Something black. No, James—no, don't pick that up. Those stones are part of the path; they belong to the church hall. Let's go over there and look at those stones; you can pick one of those up."

How had she ever thought the walk to the village shop would be a short affair? It took him half an hour just to cross the garden!

Parents and nannies were beginning to arrive with the other partygoers. Margot, who knew a few of them from church, said, "Look, there's Albert and Jane!"

Margot was a veteran of church Christmas parties, of course. It felt strange to be here as a mother, even a disguised one, like crossing an invisible boundary into adulthood. There had been none last year, of course, because of the Spanish influenza. She had thought crossing the boundary would be something that happened once, when she became an adult, but in fact it was something that had happened over and over again: when the telegram came about Harry, when she left school, when she left home, when James was born. She still felt— even now—like a child playing at being a grown-up. She might be living the trappings of a grown-up life, but she knew that if something actually grown-up happened—if Mother or Father were killed in a motorcar accident, for example, and she and Stephen had to deal with the consequences—she would be flung back onto the other side of the boundary and into childhood.

She sat at the edge of the room with the other attendants, most of whom, of course, were older than she was. Mary's nursemaid was there with Mary's eldest, Victoria— the baby was teething, she explained to Margot, so she was at home. Mary sent her regards.

As well as Victoria and James, there were a few other tiny children, including a fat baby in awful bright-pink woollies who crawled all over the floor, getting in everyone's way, and cried when anyone tried to thwart it. Its mother ignored it completely and sat as close to the oil stove as she could get, occasionally shouting at her older child to "Stop bothering me, do! Go and play!"

Margot had thought that James might be shy, but after his initial caution had worn off, he was anything but. He ran around the party, trying to join in with the older children's games, always a little behind but always eager to get it right. He danced about excitedly at blindman's bluff, thrilled to bits when he was allowed to be the blind man (though of course Jocelyn quickly allowed him to catch her, knowing from experience how soon little children got frustrated by this game). His face puckered up with concentration at grandmother's footsteps, saying "Shh! Shh!" like the other children, though it wasn't clear he understood the rules at all, and he had to be told to stop moving when Jocelyn turned around.

Watching him, in his blue flannel rompers and knitted jersey, his fair little head bobbing excitedly among the older children, Margot wondered if it was as obvious to everyone else there what a superior child he was. Look at him—so happy, so eager to join in! How intelligent he clearly was for a child not yet two and a half! How darling! One or two of the little girls with their curls and party dresses might be prettier, but he was far and away the most attractive of the little boys. So sturdy! So sweet! So happy!

How could her mother possibly think it was a comfort to tell her that she could have another child? How could another baby possibly replace this funny little person bobbing about on tiptoes with his hand in the air as Jocelyn called for volunteers for a sack race? A sack race against all these bigger boys! Jocelyn gave him a sack, and of course he came last, hopping bravely behind Ernest and Hilary Connor and Adam Jacobson. But how cheerful he seemed about the whole thing! (Of course, it was possible that he hadn't realized it *was* a race.)

How, she marveled, had someone as awful as she managed to create a little creature as wonderful as this?

It was almost enough to make one believe in God after all.

THE TROUBLE
WITH JAMES

—————•••⟫⟪•••—————

THE TROUBLE WAS, EVEN AFTER ALL THIS TIME,
Margot couldn't decide one way or the other.

Did she want a child or didn't she? Margot thought back
to the mother-and-baby home. To the girl in the bed beside
her, her breasts bound with black crepe bandages to keep
in the milk, screaming and screaming because one morning her baby simply hadn't been wheeled in with the others.
He'd been taken away to his new parents the night before.
The girl had known this was going to happen, of course.
But she thought she would be allowed to say goodbye.

When James was growing inside her, Margot had
known she was lucky. The other mothers in the home
faced a dreadful choice: a lifetime of shame or an impossible goodbye. She'd had the best of both worlds, or so she'd

thought. The very notion of a baby had terrified her, even Harry's baby, even now that Harry was gone. She had felt no connection to the thing growing inside her. She had not wanted to be a mother. She had not wanted a child. She had not wanted any of it.

But then, when he'd come. When she'd *held* him. The tininess of him. The perfection, like a cross little old man, all curled up onto himself as he lay against her stomach. The soft red skin, the fine black hair (it turned blond later). You thought of babies with curls and dimples, didn't you? James hadn't had curls or dimples—he hadn't looked anything like the babies in a Pears soap advertisement. He hadn't looked *sweet* at all. He was a *person*. She hadn't expected that. A proper warm little person.

"*Hullo,*" she'd whispered, and he'd lifted his head and mewled at her, like a kitten.

Her baby. Her *son*.

She had never wanted a baby. She'd looked at the girls—women, some of them—who were going to keep their children, and had been filled with visceral terror. To live like that! To be disbarred from polite society forever, to be hissed at and whispered at in the street, the way some of the women from the village whispered at the girls in the home. Margot's father was fond of sermonizing on the way in which God sent lessons designed for the sinner. From the vain woman, he took beauty. From the strong man, his strength. From Job, he took everything. Margot had never been able to forgive God for Job.

Margot had always thought that vanity was her weakness, but in those months in the home, cleaning the floors and tending the garden with the other girls, she'd realized that actually it was how much she cared about how others saw her. How much she wanted to be liked. If she kept this baby, she would lose everything, it seemed to her, at sixteen. A place in society. A marriage and a home of her own. Because who would marry her, knowing she had a child?

Really, she was lucky that her parents had given her a way out.

But then she'd met him. Held him. This tiny warm body, lying close and safe against her skin.

Then she'd known with absolute certainty that she wasn't lucky at all.

She had not wanted a child. Not even Harry's child. She had wanted nothing to do with the very idea of it.

But she had wanted James.

TWO O'CLOCK

HARRY RANG THE DOORBELL AT TWO O'CLOCK
precisely. Margot was helping her mother write out laundry lists, and she flinched. Her mother looked at her. "All
right?"

"Yes, thank you." Now she was going crimson, she could
feel it.

James, who was sitting on her mother's knee, dropped
his lead soldier and cried, "Dimmy!"

"He thinks it's the grocer's boy," said Margot's mother.
She kissed his blond hair. "No, darling, it's not Jimmy. It's
someone for Margot."

Ernest and Ruth, sprawled on their bellies on the floor
with a copy of *The Magnet* between them, looked up with
interest.

Edith appeared in the doorway. "Mr. Harry Singer, ma'am."

"Golly!" said Ruth, sitting up.

"All right," their mother said. She stood, lifting James onto her hip. He wriggled and put out his hands for the soldier. "Come on, Jamie, let's go upstairs. Don't *fuss*, silly boy; here he is. Ruth, I think Edith wanted some help making mince pies for the Girls' Friendly Society Christmas party."

"What? Oh, Mother, no! Let me stay!"

"Ernest, you may stay here and read quietly. Margot, I hope I can trust you and Harry."

I hope . . . Margot's face flared. She didn't think . . . she couldn't . . .

And how . . . how could she possibly say what she had to say with Ernest there?

She opened her mouth to argue, then closed it. "Yes, Mother," she said.

Her mother nodded. "Come along, Ruth."

They all got to their feet as Edith showed Harry in. He was wearing a brown tweed suit and suddenly seemed very adult. He was twenty-two. A grown-up. Of course she'd always known that, but looking at him now, she had to face the truth of it. The adolescent awkwardness was gone; he was a grown person, calm and content in his own body.

"Hullo," he said, and she found herself smiling. She had forgotten what it was like to be in the same room as him. To be the focus of his attention. Not that she deserved any of that today . . . But he *was* smiling at her, and she was sure his pleasure was genuine. It made her feel truly happy for the first time all holiday. But that was foolish, wasn't it? Perhaps *he* had a new girl now. It would be surprising if he didn't. There were so few young men nowadays; a man as whole and handsome as Harry must be in demand.

Could she really expect him to have stayed faithful for the three years they'd been apart?

Perhaps that was what this meeting was about.

His letter hadn't said *fiancé*, after all. It had said *friend*.

"Hullo," she said. She came forward—should they shake hands? Embrace? She hovered, hesitating, and Harry laughed. "It's good to see you," she said, and then blushed. "Oh, I've said it again! But it is, you know."

"And you." He *was* pleased to see her, she was certain. But there was a hesitancy there as well, a holding-back. He wasn't sure of her.

Her smile widened, spreading across her face like sunshine. He smiled too—and there they were, smiling at each other.

She turned away first, saying confusedly, "Would you like tea? I could ring for Edith . . ."

"No, thank you. Hullo, Ernest, old chap, how's tricks?"

Oh goodness, what *were* they going to talk about? He was going to ask her why she hadn't replied to his letters—of course he was—and there was Ernest, fair, stolid Ernest, his blond head studiously bent over his paper.

"How are you?" she said quickly.

"Well. I'm well. I'm going to be a farmer—did you know?"

"Yes! Your mother told me. How splendid!"

"Well, I think it is. My uncle farms, you know. He was always sorry none of his children wanted to go into it, so he's terribly pleased about me. The plan is to study agriculture next year—probably one of the northern universities. The doctors thought I wouldn't quite be fit enough this year, and I must say I'm rather glad. There are a fearful lot of army chaps going this year, and I think it would be nicer to do it properly. I've been living with my uncle in the dales, helping out with the animals, and I feel rather as though it's all my childhood holidays come at once."

"I was so sorry to hear you were ill."

Oh, surely that was the wrong thing to say! Surely his next question would be why she hadn't answered his letters?

"Yes, it was rather beastly. I was on a farm in Germany with another couple of chaps—that's what gave me the taste for it, you know. Actually, I think that probably saved my life, because the family I was working for were rather decent to me. Some prisoners had a simply frightful time—in camps and so forth—but the family we were with were . . . well, they were just ordinary people, you know, in wartime. Only we all had to work terribly hard, and there was never very much food. We were luckier than most, because there's always food on a farm, isn't there?—but Germany was fearfully hungry, at the end of the War."

"I suppose it must have been," said Margot. She thought back to last year. Margarine and no cake and rationing and queues at the fishmonger's. "I mean, we were blockading them, weren't we? That was the point."

"Well, yes," said Harry. "But if you'd been there . . . I mean, people were starving. And of course no one wants to give food to prisoners of war when children are dying. I don't suppose I would either, if it were Prissy and Mabel . . ."

"No," said Margot thoughtfully.

"So I was in pretty bad shape when I came home. Better than many people were, but still . . . The doctor chappie said I was run-down and packed me off to the Isle of Wight to a convalescent home with a whole lot of other soldiers. That was rather grim."

He made a face.

Margot said, "Oh, why?"

"Well . . . You know what soldiers are like—or maybe

you don't? It's all *jaw jaw jaw* about the War, and people they know, and campaigns they were in, and how fearful it all was. One feels rather a fool when one spent the whole War at school or starving on a dairy farm in Bavaria."

"That does sound rather beastly." Margot smiled at him. She was remembering all the things she liked about him. She knew exactly what he meant about the soldiers—all Stephen's friends, talking endlessly about the War.

There was an awkward pause—the first in the whole conversation.

Harry said, "And—and what about you? How have you been? You said you were a typist."

"Yes, in a girls' school in Durham. I work in the office, typing up letters and telephoning the parents to tell them Joan's feeling unwell. It's an awful bore."

"And I suppose you have a new chap now?"

It was said casually, but she could see that he was anything but casual.

"I don't, actually," she said as calmly as she could. "I haven't had anything like that in a long time. Not since you went to France."

She watched him take in this information. He had always been terrible at hiding his feelings.

"Oh!" he said. Then a smile spread over his face. "Oh . . ."

"And you?" she said. "It's been nearly three years, surely . . . I mean, I have read novels, I know that soldiers—"

And I didn't reply to those letters.

"Oh well." He looked awkward.

He had another girl. Of course he did. There were so few young men left now, and one as—well, as eligible as Harry—of *course* he had another girl.

"When you didn't—I—I confess I was rather cut up about it, and—"

She said hurriedly, "Oh no, of course. That's wonderful, Harry. I'm very happy for you; you deserve every—every—"

"Oh!" He was—was he *laughing*? "No, it wasn't . . . I'm not . . . it was nothing like that!"

"Then what . . . ?"

"Well . . ." A glance at Ernest, his fair head still bent over *The Magnet*. "Look here, it was just—I was rather upset, and there was a VAD girl—it wasn't anything, honor bright."

It wasn't anything. Had he—had they? She couldn't ask. But the thought suddenly blinded her with misery. Lovely Harry Singer, moving easily through the world like a scythe through corn, leaving girls behind him like . . . like . . . baby field mice torn from their nests? Perhaps not. Something like that, anyway. Lovely Harry Singer—he wasn't lovely at all if he could say "It wasn't anything" about *that*.

"I say!" Something of this must have been showing on

her face. "Really, it wasn't—wasn't anything worth talking about. She never meant anything to me—"

"Never meant anything to you!" She was suddenly furious. "It's all right for you to say that—disappearing off to your fancy uncle's farm. What about her?"

"Now, look here—"

"You're all the same, all of you! You can do whatever you like, and nobody gives a fig! It's the women who have to live with it when you're gone!"

"Good lord!" He was looking at her like she'd started speaking in tongues. "I just took the girl dancing a couple of times! I didn't break her heart! If we're going to talk about disappearing, what about you? Nine months I've been home, and you haven't so much as written! I thought you must be engaged to another chap and couldn't face telling me! And now you tell me it isn't that—so what is it, Margot? Because I haven't got a bloody clue!"

He was really angry. She couldn't remember ever seeing him like this before. She stared, shocked. His face was flushed and furious. His chest was heaving. She suddenly, shockingly, wanted nothing more than to kiss him, full on the lips.

"I can't!" she said. "I wish I could, but I can't—not here—" She looked across at Ernest, who had lowered *The Magnet* and was staring at them in amazement. "And I couldn't—not in a letter either. And not in a hospital with your mother there chaperoning us!"

His mouth was moving. She wondered what he was thinking. Did he—had he *guessed*? It seemed so clear to her, but perhaps it was like reading a murder mystery, like one of the Sexton Blake stories. The solution was always so obvious, the second time you read it . . .

"What the devil?" he said.

Obviously not.

She was nearly crying.

"I'm sorry!" she cried. "I'm so sorry!"

He moved toward her.

"Look here—I didn't . . ."

But all of a sudden she couldn't bear it. The sympathy in his eyes, and what would he think if he knew the truth?

"Oh, don't!" she cried.

She pushed past him and rushed across the hall and up the stairs, while he stood gaping in astonishment.

FOUR WEEKS

------◆·◆·◆·》》《·◆·◆·◆------

HE'D BEEN HERS FOR FOUR WEEKS.

Four weeks in the home. A warm body, sleeping on her stomach like a little monkey.

They'd kept the babies in another room from the mothers, wheeling them in when it was time to feed, wheeling them out again afterward. But James had known who she was. She was sure of it. Could babies hear things from inside the womb? Could they recognize their mother's voice when they came out into the world? He had stirred when she spoke to him, in a way he hadn't for the nurses. She used to whisper his name to him while he suckled. She had named him. If her parents had wanted to call him something different, they hadn't said anything.

She could make him stop crying when nobody else could. He had known her.

Had he missed her when she'd left? Did he think she'd abandoned him?

He was perfection. Perfect face. Perfect eyes, perfect tiny, soft red hands and feet. Perfect smooth cheeks and tiny, perfect eyelashes.

Somewhere, there was another Margot who had raised him herself. Who had scooped him up in her arms and walked out the door, who was living in a little house, just James and her. Paying the rent by . . . but here Margot's imagination ran out. Taking in washing? Sewing shirts? They were despised by the world, but they did not care, because they had each other.

Somewhere, there was another Margot who had waited until marriage like a good girl should, and had delivered her firstborn in her marital bed and loved him best of all for the rest of her life.

She hadn't known it would be like this.

She hadn't known you could love something like that. It wasn't rational. It had come from nowhere, this animal urge to protect him, to be near him. It wasn't love exactly— it didn't feel like love. It felt like something beyond her, outside her, something she wasn't able to control.

It had frightened her a little.

He was the most beautiful thing she had ever seen. She didn't think she would be able to give him away. When it came down to it, she had been sure she would change her mind and refuse to sign the papers. Letting him go would be an abomination against nature and against the Will of God. She wouldn't allow it to happen.

But she had.

THE MARRIED LADY
AT HOME

MARY AND GEORGE LIVED AT THE VERY END OF A
row of terraced houses. It was a respectable street on the
edge of the village. The stone flags and the windows were
well scrubbed, but Mary's curtains were threadbare, and
although her window was cheerful with a Christmas tree
and paper chains, the decorations were clearly Woolworth's
finest. Though not quite four o'clock, the sun was already
setting, a dull reddish glow through the low clouds. The
lamplighter was making his way down the street. Smoke
was rising from the chimney pots, and on the corner a gaggle of small boys were playing cricket against a gable end.

Mary answered the doorbell, baby on her hip and
Victoria clutching her skirts. Mary's hair was falling down,
and there was a streak of soot across her cheek. She said,

"Darling! How splendid to see you! Come in! You'll just have to shut your eyes and pretend everything's in order—it's Eliza's half-day, and I gave Gladys a week off for Christmas. George says I was a fool, and I expect he's right, but she did so want to go home, and her mother lost both sons in the War, so naturally one wants to be kind." She paused for breath. "She lives in Barnsley, you see. Gladys's mother, I mean, so it isn't as though Gladys could go there and back in a day. And I thought, well, what sort of mother would I be if I couldn't manage the children for a week— Oh, darling! I didn't mean!"

"It's quite all right," said Margot. She kissed Mary. "I'm not a bit offended, and I don't know how you begin to manage the girls without a nursemaid, even for a week."

"Well, darling, between you and me, neither do I. The woman who does my washing has *nine*—can you imagine? Nine children, and no sort of help, of course. *And* she's a washerwoman. I barely have time to wash my own hands, and— Yes, darling, what is it?" This to Victoria, whose tugging on her skirts was growing too insistent to be ignored. "Well, *I* don't know! You'll have to ask her yourself, won't you?" Victoria retreated farther behind her mother. "Though actually, dear, it's rather rude to ask people if they have a Christmas present for you. What if she didn't? Imagine how awkward it would be!"

"But fortunately I do, so all our feelings are spared," said Margot. "Shall we go inside and see what it is?"

••••• →)((← •••••

THE LITTLE FRONT ROOM WAS, AS MARY HAD SAID, in a state of some chaos. Victoria's wooden horse was lying on its side on the hearth rug, its wheeled legs in the air. Mary's workbox was open on the side table, its scissors halfway through turning a copy of the *Illustrated London News* into strings of paper dolls. Victoria's colored pencils were spread out over the tea table, along with an open jar of jam, a ball of wool, a stuffed bear, a teething ring, and a box of cigarettes.

"Darling, I know!" said Mary as Margot took in all this and more: the bookcase made out of orange crates, the mismatched armchairs, the magazines and letters and children's pictures piled on the floor, the picture leaning against the wall still waiting to be hung. "But you don't know what it's like! I start every day with the best of intentions, and somehow nothing ever seems to get done."

"I think it's perfectly charming," said Margot. She was noticing other details now: the cheap baubles on the Christmas tree all shining in the gaslight, the tiny candles waiting to be lit, the strings of paper chains hanging from the sconces.

Mary was one of the very few people she'd told about James—just Mary; Mary's husband, George; and Jos and Stephen. After she'd realized she was in trouble, she'd felt so . . . *distant* from her school friends. What did the sixth form know about babies? But Mary was different. Mary was nineteen and married with a new baby of her own. She hadn't had a house then—she'd been living with her mother while George was in France—but Margot knew she could talk to her. That Mary would understand, wouldn't goggle at her or tell the other girls. Would know what it meant to have a child, and what it might mean to lose one.

Later, she had clung to Mary a little. She couldn't help herself. It was a form of self-torture—look what you could have had, if you'd been more careful, if you'd been braver— but also, oddly, a comfort. She had drifted apart from her school friends, although now they were older, they might have more in common. Most of them had jobs now, and one or two had fiancés.

Friendship with any of the girls in the boardinghouse was impossible. Mary's was one of the few places in her life where she could be honest.

"Now, Victoria, what do I have in here . . . ?"

The children's presents were duly distributed; the baby dressed in her new jacket and admired, Victoria's tea set ("Margot, you *shouldn't* have!") unpacked, and Bear and

Mary and Margot all served imaginary tea with imaginary milk and paper biscuits. Then Victoria discovered that *she* was hungry too, and Baby was handed to Aunty Margot ("She's a perfect duck, thank heavens") while Mary disappeared into the kitchen. She soon reappeared with a huge brown teapot full of tea and a plate of muffins, which they toasted on the fire. Then Baby, who'd been growing increasingly fretful, began to wail, and Mary settled down in the chair by the fire to nurse. Margot lit all the little candles on the Christmas tree, carefully supervised by Victoria to make sure she didn't miss a single one.

"What do you think?" she asked Victoria.

"Stu-pen-dous!" said the little girl, and the adults laughed.

"But, darling, how are things *really*?" said Margot as Victoria settled down to make tea for Bear and two rag dolls.

"Oh well. I know I shouldn't complain, and we're very lucky, really. But goodness, it is hard work! We only have Eliza mornings, you see, and of course the rough work takes most of her time—I really *couldn't* do that—so it does leave rather a lot. And I always was a perfect dunce at domestic science. Gladys does her best, but she's only fifteen, so she does need everything explained rather, and she tends to think Baby needs feeding when really it's only wind. And of course one never knows if George is going to be in or out."

"Yes, how *is* George?"

George had been in the Royal Army Medical Corps but had been sent home in 1917 with nervous exhaustion.

"Oh—ever so much better. He's such a good doctor, everyone says so. But he does *worry*."

"How so?"

"Oh well—like Mrs. Higgins's little boy. They really thought he would die, and though I don't like to say so, Dr. Singer said he thought he *would* have died if it hadn't been for George. But George says he won't ever walk, and he may not talk. George can't help but think—if he'd had more experience of childbirth, you know . . ."

"But surely nobody thinks . . ."

"Oh! Of course nobody does. But he will keep going to see them, and he won't think of charging, and the mother is so grateful, which just makes everything worse. I'm afraid," she confessed with a pathetic air of apology, "George is in the habit of picking up charity patients. The local people know he won't charge if they can't pay, and word has gotten around, rather."

"Father's just the same," said Margot, thinking of the "poor cupboard" by the stairs and the lonely people at Christmas.

"And of course it's all very noble of him; I don't say it isn't," Mary went on hurriedly. "Only—well, the butcher

does need paying, doesn't he? And the girls will have to be educated somehow, and goodness, Margot, I never knew how expensive children were until I had my own! Victoria goes through shoes as quick as blinking! I'm sure we never used to grow so fast."

"It does sound rather worrying."

"Well, it is. But there! It isn't anything like what some families have to go through. When I think of the men who came home blinded or with such terrible wounds—look at Lionel Parker, say, or Reggie Fletcher. Or those who didn't come home at all.

"And of course I wouldn't trade George and the children for the world," she finished, with something of the air of a women's magazine.

"Hmm," said Margot. "The world isn't all it's cracked up to be."

"Oh dear! Here I am going on and on about us, and I haven't *begun* to ask about you."

"Oh well. There isn't really very much to say. I just go on the same as ever I always did."

There was a short silence, broken only by Victoria. "Would you yike a cake, Bear? Yes, pease! All right, here you go. Sank you! Would you yike another cake? No, sank you."

Mary said very carefully, "If you'd just *talk* to Harry . . ."

"And say what?"

"I know he still loves you . . ."

Margot gave a short bark of a laugh.

"No," she said. "How can he possibly love me? Could *you* love George if he'd done what I did to—to Victoria? If you'd gone all these years living this other life, and all the time Victoria was there and nobody had told you she even *existed?*"

Mary drew in her breath.

"You see? It's not so simple."

"But darling, you *couldn't* tell him. You didn't even know he was alive."

"I've known since February," said Margot.

"Well, that isn't so very long. And he was on the Isle of Wight, and—"

"The postal service does reach the Isle of Wight, you know. It isn't entirely cut off from civilization."

Another pause.

"Why didn't you tell him?"

"Oh . . ." Margot twisted her head from side to side. "It was such a shock, him being still alive! The telegram they sent just said *Missing in action*, so of course we all thought he was dead. And then in February I got a cable from his mother saying he was alive and coming home. I just didn't know what to say. Then she sent me this letter about how he had pneumonia and how ill he'd been and would I go and see him? And—" She stopped. "I funked it," she said simply. "They never let us be together without a chaperone, and I thought, how *could* I tell him with his mother there? And how could I write it in a letter? It wasn't him who wrote, you see, it was his mother, so I thought he must be so ill that she was reading his letters to him. And if she found out . . . well, it would all be over for James and my parents, wouldn't it? But how could I write to him if I hadn't told him? What would I say? It would be starting the whole thing off on a lie, and . . . I've been lying for so long, and I hate it more than anything. I couldn't bear the thought of lying to him, even by omission."

"But what did you say to his mother?"

Margot looked at her hands. "I never wrote either of them back. After an age, Harry sent me a letter. He sent me a couple, actually. Quite decent letters, considering. But by then it was too late. I just didn't know what to say. And now—well, it *is* too late, isn't it? It must be."

"I think," said Mary thoughtfully, "that now is the time—this holiday, I mean. You're here and he's here and there'll be parties and things where you won't be chaperoned, won't there? There always are. I think you behaved like a bloody fool, but I think it's just *about* forgivable—now. But if you leave it any longer, it won't be. You'll just have to go your way and he go his, and that's that. When are you going back to that awful school?"

"The fourth of January."

"Well, there you are. You have to decide what you want, darling. And you've got till the end of the holidays to do it."

STEPHEN

---◉▶◀◉---

IT WAS DARK AS MARGOT WALKED HOME THROUGH
the village, the stars appearing one by one over the roof-
tops. Every little house was lit up, Christmas trees in the
windows, smoke rising from the chimneys, and the air that
glorious mixture of coal smoke and dirt and frost.

As she opened the front door, she closed her eyes and
breathed in the familiar smells of home—linoleum and coal
and tobacco and wet umbrellas. This was a good home. It
had been a good childhood, on the whole. She was glad
this home would be her son's.

By the sound of it, everyone was in the drawing room.
Ruth's high, excitable voice and a familiar male laugh.
Stephen. The prodigal son was home.

She took off her coat, unpinned her hat, and hung

them on the coat stand. Then she opened the drawing-room door.

They were all sitting around the fire, the tea still spread out on the table. The children were playing a noisy game of snap. James was watching with fascination, laughing every time Ruth or Ernest shouted "Snap!" and joining in. Stephen was sitting on the hearth rug, arranging chestnuts on the coal shovel. Jocelyn had her embroidery on her lap, but she was smiling. And Mother—Mother was sitting in the chair by the fireside, her whole face aglow with joy.

"Margot!" she cried.

"Hullo, Stephen," said Margot with a smile. She liked her brother.

"Hullo, old thing," said Stephen, getting to his feet.

They embraced. He looked tired, she thought, watching his face with an odd quickening of anxiety. Stephen had had a hard War too. He'd gone to France in 1917. But while Harry had been captured almost immediately, Stephen had spent eighteen months in uniform, first in the trenches, then as a driver for one of the generals.

He'd been discharged in March and seemed happy enough, if rather distant. He'd always been a bit awkward, fairly musical—he played piano and sang in the church choir—without ever being exceptional. There'd been some idea of him becoming a schoolmaster, and he had agreed to teach piano and singing in a boys' prep school without enthusiasm. The post had lasted less than a month. The headmaster complained that Stephen was often late—sleeping past breakfast and missing choir practice and seeming to forget his turn at taking prep. The situation had come to a head three weeks in, when he'd gone to the local pub with a couple of the other younger teachers, ex-soldiers all—and, the headmaster seemed to imply, rather struggling to integrate into civilian life. They'd come back roaring drunk at midnight, singing soldiers' songs outside the junior boys' dormitory and splashing about in the fountain.

This had been a huge shock to Stephen's family. Stephen was basically a good child—awkward, yes, and idiosyncratic definitely, occasionally vehement (there'd been a teacher at his prep school who'd mistakenly punished one child for another's mistakes, and Stephen was so furious he refused to speak to him for the rest of the year). But basically clever and good-hearted.

"Darling, *why?*" their mother had wailed, and Stephen had shrugged.

His father found him a junior place in an accountancy firm in Sheffield.

"Is that all right?" he'd said in his mild way, and Stephen had shrugged again.

The accountancy firm had lasted a little longer—until the end of August. Their father, on writing to his friend, discovered more of the same sort of thing. Stephen spent much of his time sleeping at his desk, doodling on the back of invoices, and reading detective novels instead of working. His father worked on another of his endless contacts, and since October, Stephen had been with a tea merchant in Leeds. Margot wondered how long this place was going to last.

"Oh!" said their mother, watching them now. "Isn't it heavenly to have everyone at home at last! Our first Christmas all together since the War!"

Stephen winced.

The evening passed as usual. Ruth and Ernest had supper in the nursery with James. Ruth ate with the adults in term time but preferred to eat upstairs with Ernest during the holidays. The children were expected to change for the evening, though—they dressed after supper and came down to the drawing room to sit with their parents for an hour.

James, of course, went to bed first. Then Ernest and Ruth, at eight, then their father, who began nodding over his Trollope at about nine o'clock. Their mother sat with the older children for a while longer, but at last she too rose and made her way upstairs, leaving Stephen, Margot, and Jocelyn alone.

They looked at one another a little curiously, a little shyly.

Stephen sat back in his chair, the fingers of his right hand plucking at the back of his left. Margot thought he looked much older than his twenty-one years. His skin had a grayish tinge to it.

"Thank goodness for that," he said. "I'm not sure I could bear any more bonhomie, could you?" He jumped up, went over to the cabinet in the corner of the room, and crouched beside it. "Drink, anyone?"

"All right," Margot said. She was nineteen now; she ought to be old enough, oughtn't she? Especially at Christmas.

"Good girl. Sherry? Whisky? Brandy? Port—good God, the Pater hasn't left this open since last Christmas, has he? He ought to be shot."

"Er—whisky, please, I think," Margot said. "Sherry sounds so maiden-auntish."

"Rather. What about you, Jos?"

Jocelyn hesitated. Margot wondered if Stephen remembered how young she was. Then, "I'll have sherry, please. I'm likely to be a maiden aunt no matter what I do, so I may as well enjoy it."

"Rot! If I wasn't a blood relation, I'd marry you like a shot, and so would any chap with sense."

"It's all right, Steve, you needn't play nice for the

children. I'm quite resigned to it. There are two million spare women in Britain; don't you read the newspapers? And if anyone was ever a spare woman, it's me. I just need to decide what I'm going to do instead."

"Crikey. You aren't going to be a policewoman like Ruth, are you?"

"No. But I only have one life, and I don't intend to waste it." She gave him a pointed look. "Unlike some people I could name."

Stephen winced. "Mea culpa. Don't you start. It's going to be bad enough when the Pater finds out—" He stopped.

Jocelyn cried, "Finds out? Oh, Steve! Not again. What happened?"

"Let him pour the drinks before you start the third degree, can't you?" said Margot.

Stephen bowed. There was a pause while he filled the glasses and handed them around.

"Here," he said. "To us all. And to Christmas."

"To Christmas."

They drank. Margot tried not to make a face. The whisky tasted like fire and medicine. Stephen caught her eye and winked, and she resisted the urge to throw her glass at him.

"Now," she said. "Steve, old boy. Tell us all. You didn't set fire to the boss's trousers, did you?"

"Don't be ridiculous." He shook his head. "It was nothing. I'm more interested in Jocelyn here. If she isn't going to be a policewoman, what *is* she going to be? How about an explorer?"

"Or a lady archaeologist," said Margot, joining in the fun.

Jocelyn frowned.

"You needn't twit," she said. "It's all right for you. Men can be anything. And it's not as though Margot need worry. It isn't a bit the same for girls—"

"Hold up," said Margot. "Why needn't I worry?" She felt obliquely hurt. "I'm not going to stay in that beastly school forever."

"Oh! I didn't mean that." Jocelyn looked surprised. "Only that you'll marry, of course. If not Harry, then someone else. It isn't like *you* need worry about men being interested."

"I don't know that that's so certain." Margot was unsure whether to be insulted or flattered by this. "It's not as though I ever meet any eligible men—even if I wanted to— which I'm not saying I *do* . . ."

"Oh dry up," said Stephen. "Of course you'll marry Harry. And if you don't, you're a damn fool, that's all."

"Lay off," said Jocelyn with a glance at Margot. "I don't see that you're in any position to cast nasturtiums. What are you doing with your life? Getting the boot from one job after another, as far as I can see."

"Yes," said Margot. "What *did* happen, Steve? You can tell us."

"Oh, it wasn't anything," said Stephen again. He looked suddenly shifty. He began playing with a box of matches on the table. "Just . . ." He looked from one sister to the other, then: "Don't you ever wonder what the *point* of it all is?"

"Yes," said Margot, at the same time as Jocelyn said "No."

They looked at each other and laughed.

"Don't you, Jos? Good for you. I wonder why not?"

"I'm a vicar's daughter, aren't I?" Jocelyn tucked her hair behind her ears. Even with it up, she still looked a child. Her serious little sister. "It goes with the territory. Even if I don't believe in—well, God and all that."

"Goodness, don't you?"

"No, I don't think so." Jocelyn was serious. "At least— I don't *know* that I do. Not like Father. But that doesn't mean I don't think men like Father have the right way of looking at the world. We can blow one another to bits and gas ourselves to death or we can—well, try and help each other, like Mother and Father do. *That's* the point, isn't it? The only one that matters, anyway."

"Soup kitchens and whatnot?"

"And whatnot." Jocelyn looked from her brother to her sister. "*Don't* laugh! I'm serious."

"I know you are." Stephen looked at her affectionately. "I'm all for compassion. I just . . . well, it isn't so easy in practice, is it?"

"Nothing ever is," said Jocelyn. She leaned forward, her thin hands clutching each other. "I wish I *did* believe in God," she said. "Then I could be a nun. I always rather liked the idea of being a nun. It seems so *simple*."

"Never trust anyone who makes out life is simple," said Stephen darkly. "France was supposed to be simple. Duty and honor and all that. And look where it led us."

"Poor old Steve," said Margot. She took another glug of her whisky. "I'm with you. You do what's supposed to be the right thing, and it all goes to pot. Let's stick to wickedness; it's a damn sight easier, and at least we all know where we stand."

"Amen!" Stephen raised his glass. They drank. "Poor old Pater. At least one of his children turned out all right."

"Give her time," said Margot.

She rather thought Jocelyn might surprise them all.

CHRISTMAS EVE

AND THEN IT WAS CHRISTMAS EVE.

Father was busy, of course, preparing for the celebrations tomorrow. The house was full of expectation and excitement—cooking smells coming from the kitchen, shouts from the children, people disappearing into rooms to write Christmas cards and wrap presents and plan complicated secrets.

There was a trip to a nearby copse to cut mistletoe and holly and ivy, and a great deal of enthusiasm about making paper chains and hanging holly around all the gas jets.

Her father was run off his feet, but every Christmas Eve, without fail, he gave up most of the morning to make gingerbread biscuits with the children. Margot had always loved this tradition and had always intended to do the same thing with her own children. She wandered down to the kitchen, half-intending to help, but it was clear she was not wanted.

Ernest and Ruth were enthusiastically rolling out the dough. Both were covered in flour, and Ernest had a streak of what looked like cinnamon across his cheek.

James was sitting on her father's knee. He had a cookie cutter in his hand, and her father was showing him how to press it into the dough.

"That's right, old man," he said. "Look! A star!"

"Tar," said James.

"That's right. And then we'll put it in the oven, and when it comes out, it'll be a star cookie!"

"Tar ookie!"

"Good man."

Margot felt a strange lump in her chest, somewhere between grief and envy.

Look what you're giving him, she told herself fiercely. *Just look at him! He'd never have a Christmas like this with you, would he?*

She retreated up to the bedroom she shared with Jocelyn and spread her Christmas presents out on the bed. Nothing very fancy. Handkerchiefs for the adults in the family.

Chocolates for the children. The extra bits she'd picked up at the grocer's. And James . . .

James's present had been difficult. The youngest child in a large household never exactly *wants* for toys; the day nursery was full of twenty years' worth of train sets and dollhouses and Noah's arks and balls and bricks and tricycles. Not so many new toys, of course; the War had made that difficult. But that didn't matter so much to a small child.

Margot had agonized over the choices in the toy shop. A teddy bear? They had a lovely one with a stiff, funny snout. But was James the sort of child who cared for teddy bears? His interests had been mechanical the last time she'd seen him—cars and trains and boats. There were some lovely trains in the toy shop, but they were aimed at rather older children, and Margot and the shopgirl agreed they would be wasted on a two-year-old. In the end she bought him a wooden ship. It was too old for him, but the toys for younger children looked so *dull*. She could still remember her own childhood excitement at older children's toys.

The Christmas stocking had been more fun. The Allen children always had their first stocking at two, and Margot had enjoyed the challenge of finding as many things that would fit as she could. Candy canes. Sugar mice. A toy trumpet, a wind-up mouse, nuts, an orange, of course, and a little woolly dog to sit on the top.

But when she had presented the stocking to her mother, she could see at once that it was a mistake.

"*You've* done him a stocking?" her mother had said, and Margot realized with a crashing sense of her own idiocy that *of course* her mother would have made James a stocking. Why on earth wouldn't she?

"It's a lovely idea, darling," her mother said with some bewilderment, looking at the little collection of things. "But that's about twice as much as Ruth and Ernest have. Stockings are supposed to come from Father Christmas, though I don't suppose either of the older two really believe in him anymore. But they'll mind dreadfully if he favors one child over the others. Surely you can see that?"

Margot's cheeks flamed. "I suppose—I didn't—"

"And the stocking gifts are supposed to be a set," her mother went on. "They've all got new flannels, and little purses that a lady in the parish sewed for them. Doris and James wrote a letter to Father Christmas and posted it up the chimney. James said he wanted a whistle, so your father's given him that old one they used to use for the games at the Sunday School Treat."

"Of course," said Margot humbly. "I should have thought. I just . . ." To her horror, she felt tears coming into her eyes. She had given James to her mother and father. Hadn't she?

So why couldn't she let him go?

In the end, they'd agreed on a compromise—dividing the presents somewhat evenly among the three stockings. The ship would be Margot's own gift to James. Margot wrapped this up now and put the whole collection into her shopping bag, ready for the Christmas tree.

She then went over to her desk and looked at the Christmas cards all addressed and waiting to be posted. There was one for Harry still unwritten.

What to say?

Even if he didn't—didn't want her . . . surely he deserved to know about James?

Or would it be kinder to leave him in ignorance?

She had left the Christmas card on the table since yesterday. But now she could hear Mary's voice in the back of her head. *I think that now is the time . . .*

"Oh damn!" she said out loud, and reached for the ink bottle. Dipping her pen into the ink, she wrote, without thinking too hard about it:

Dear Harry,

    Happy Christmas. I am frightfully sorry about storming out like that. I know I was an ass. Please understand that I have good reason to be, and it isn't something I can talk about in front of Ernest.

    Christmas is all about forgiveness, so I hope you can find it in yourself to forgive,

Your affectionate friend,
Margot

There!

MIDNIGHT

CHRISTMAS EVE. THE CHRISTMAS EVE DINNER eaten, the overexcited children put to bed, their father and mother dispatched to Midnight Mass. Margot had wondered about going too, but in the end had decided on an early night.

And now . . .

A clanging, a clashing, a tolling, a ringing.

Margot surfaced, rising from the depths of a sleep so total it still clogged her senses. She'd been dreaming. Something about Harry and something hidden in the walls—a dead man, or was it an animal? No, it had gone, she couldn't remember it. Something awful, anyway. And now this noise . . .

"What is it?" she said groggily, and from Jocelyn's side

of the room she heard fumbling, then the spark of a match. A candle flared.

"It's the bells," Jocelyn said. "For Christmas morning. They couldn't ring them last year—I suppose they didn't have the men."

The Christmas bells. They rang them at the end of Midnight Mass—of course they did. Only somewhere in the middle of the War, they'd stopped ringing all of the bells—the passing bells for the dead, the wedding bells for the living, even the church bells on Sunday mornings. And all the bell ringers had gone to war . . .

And now the men were home, and they were ringing in Christmas.

From the nursery, she could hear crying. Doris was at Mass . . . but before she could move, Jocelyn was up and past her, heading for the nursery, clutching the candlestick.

James was standing up in his cot, clinging to the side and sobbing. Jocelyn stroked his back. Margot caught him up in her arms, but she could not comfort him.

"He does this if he wakes up suddenly in the night—he'll be all right," said Jocelyn.

"Mummy!" James was crying, pushing her away.

"Let me try," said Jocelyn. She took James from Margot's arms and rocked him gently. "It's all right, darling; Jocelyn's here. It's only the silly bells. They won't hurt you."

"Oh, why won't they stop?" said Margot furiously.

Little faces appeared at the door, orange in the light of a new candlestick. Ruth and Ernest.

"What is it?" said Ernest wonderingly.

"It's Christmas," said Jocelyn. "There, darling, there."

"It's a beastly racket, whatever it is," said Ruth.

James wouldn't calm while those awful bells were ringing, surely? But miraculously, he seemed to. His head drooped onto Jocelyn's shoulder, and his eyes closed. Watching them, Margot felt her loss like a physical pain, somewhere over her heart.

"It's only because he knows me," said Jocelyn.

"Of course," said Margot stiffly. "It's quite all right."

"What's all right?" said Ruth. Nobody answered. "What?"

"Everything," said Jocelyn. She laid James gently back into the cot and draped the blanket over him. He didn't stir. "There!" she said. "And it's Christmas Day!"

OPENINGS

---✦❖✦---

CHRISTMAS DAY.

Stockings in the drawing room. This year, only Ruth, Ernest, and James had stockings, but everyone gathered to watch them open them anyway, Stephen grumbling about the early morning. "Really . . . Do we *have* to be up at such an ungodly hour?"

"Of course!" said Margot's mother. Margot could read the anxiety in her face. Stephen home for Christmas. All those awful wartime Christmases, not knowing where he was and if he was safe, all those prayers for his safe return. But what to do with him now that he was home? "Think of the children!" she said, and Stephen groaned and muttered something that made Margot's mother tighten her lips and seem to swallow a retort.

Margot, though she tried not to show it, was excited about the stockings. James's first!

"Happy Christmas, Jamie-o!" she said, and he mumbled, "Happy Christmas," and went straight over to the fireplace.

Doris said, "Oh careful, Master James—wait for Doris. He loves that nutcracker," she said over her shoulder to Margot. "He'd just play with it all morning if he were allowed. There you go, darling, let Doris help you—that's right."

The nutcracker was an old-fashioned soldier boy, like the one in the ballet. He had been left on the hearth by the basket of Christmas nuts.

Margot said, "Should he have that—is it safe?"

"Oh, it's right enough if I help him," said Doris. "There you go, pet! I expect there'll be some nuts of your own in the stocking."

There were. Nuts and fruit and all sorts of lovely things, but James didn't seem to understand how stockings were supposed to work. The woolly dog was cuddled and had to be introduced to the rest of the family—Ruth and Ernest shook its paw solemnly while James said, "Woof, woof, woof!" and dissolved into giggles.

This seemed likely to go on all morning, so Margot, growing impatient, said, "Look, Jamie-o, there's a sugar mouse."

James had never seen a sugar mouse before, so that had to be explained too, and then eaten—not crunched down, like Ruth's, but solemnly sucked. Ruth and Ernest, meanwhile, had worked their way to the bottom of their own stockings and were taking an interest in James's.

"Come *on*," Ruth said, waving the stocking tantalizingly under his nose. Her voice took on the special cadence the older children adopted when mimicking the adults to their younger siblings. "Look, Jamie-o, it's full of lovely presents. Don't you want to see what's inside?"

"I'll open it for you if you want," said Ernest, practical as ever, as the grown-ups howled.

"Ernest!"

And then her father came home from the early-morning communion service and lifted him onto his knee with an easy "Come on, Jamie. Let's not keep the troops waiting, eh?"

Margot watched them, her father's hands helping James to lift the things out of the stocking, and had to look away. Her eye caught her mother's, standing in the doorway. Her mother, watching Margot, watching her father, watching James. And James, engrossed in his new whistle, unaware of them all.

At last they were finished and family prayers were over. And they were clattering into the dining room for Christmas breakfast.

"Ham!" Ruth cried as Edith brought the platters in. "Ham and eggs! Oh, angel Edith!"

"Goodness, Edith," said their mother. "Wherever did you find it?"

"I have my ways, ma'am," said Edith rather stiffly. Then, seeing the vicar's face, "My sister's husband's sister—her that was Susan Jacobs, ma'am, before she was married—well, she works at a pig farm, ma'am, and, well, you see . . ."

"Yes, all right, thank you, Edith," said Margot's mother hastily. "This is a real treat, no matter how you got it. Do tell—er—your sister's sister-in-law that we're very grateful."

"I don't think I realized until I came home how scarce grub was back here," Stephen said conversationally, stabbing a slice of fried ham with his fork and transferring it to his plate. "We always had heaps to eat on the Front—that was the one good thing about it."

"Why, you beast!" said Ruth. "And to think of all those food parcels we sent you!"

There was a small pile of Christmas cards by Margot's plate. She opened them idly while the household relaxed into its usual breakfast chaos. Nothing from Harry. Most were from old school friends, a couple from colleagues at St. Anne's. They were full of the usual dull stuff.

The card on the bottom of the stack was postmarked Newcastle, which was a surprise. She didn't think she knew anybody in Newcastle.

Dear Margot,

Writing cards this year has been somewhat diffi-cult, as you can imagine, but at least to YOU I shall need to make no explanations. YOU will understand how very, very happy I am to be able to wish you a merry Christmas and to sign this,

John, Phyllis, and Robert Backhouse

(Née Harrison. Phyllis, I mean. John was née Backhouse of course. Apologies—I am not making any sense, but I am so very, very happy. Everything is marvelous. You must come and see us! Robbie is the most delightful child in the world and I am the happi-est woman in creation.)

Margot put down the card. Her hand was shaking slightly.

"Everything all right, dear?" her mother said—damn mothers, shouldn't they have better things to do on Christmas morning than notice their daughters?

"Oh! Yes! Perfectly all right, thanks," she said, and took a gulp of tea to hide her confusion.

Phyllis. Funny, flustery, weepy little Phyllis, with her feathery hair and her way of winning the kindness of the Churchy Ladies who came to sit with them at the mother-and-baby home. The women were supposed to lecture them, Margot supposed, but like her father's own Churchy Ladies, they were rather a soft touch and spent more time cuddling the babies than worrying the mothers.

Phyllis had been a favorite of them all, with her tears, and her obvious adoration of her little boy, and her fiancé killed on the Front Line. She and Margot had become friends, mostly because they came from similar backgrounds. The majority of the other inmates were shopgirls and servants. Phyllis was a clergyman's daughter and had been living at home and working at a village school when she found herself in trouble.

Phyllis's parents had been adamant that the baby be adopted. Phyllis had acquiesced—or at least, Margot suspected, had not protested too hard. But when the baby himself arrived, Phyllis had fallen for him at once. She wept to everyone who would listen: how *could* she give him away, how could she possibly?

"Keep him, then, ducks," Norma, in the next bed, said. "Who cares what they want? If they don't want my Elsie, I don't want them; that's what I says." Norma was practical, cheerful, and completely unrepentant. She didn't even know the name of her daughter's father and had made no attempt to find out. She and Baby Elsie were going to "do" for a broad-minded lady who needed a cook-general and who, Margot rather suspected, would be getting a very good deal for her money. Norma looked like a hard worker, baby notwithstanding.

But Phyllis had other considerations. There were her parents, for one thing, to whom she was stubbornly loyal and whose comfortable lives would be devastated by an illegitimate grandson. And her own job as a school-teacher.

"Not that I *care* about that, but I'd have to support him *somehow*, wouldn't I?"

She would. And Phyllis—as both she and Margot could see quite clearly—was not the sort who could live the life Norma was proposing with any equanimity.

"It would be too *Anna Karenina*," she'd told Margot. "And I would end up resenting him—and I simply couldn't bear that. I think Mummy resented me sometimes," she'd added with a clarity that astonished Margot. "She was an artist, you know, before she married Daddy. Of course all that had to stop when Daddy and I came along. And—well, it did make for rather a beastly childhood sometimes, feel-ing like one had taken all that away from her. I'd simply hate for Robert to feel like that. Wouldn't you?"

"I suppose so," said Margot, who had never thought of her parents as people like that, with their own lives and griefs. In the end, Phyllis had refused to sign the adoption papers, and the baby had been sent to a foster family in the next village along.

"Like Cosette," said Margot doubtfully, thinking of *Les Misérables*. She didn't think it sounded like much of a life.

"Oh no!" said Phyllis. "Not like Cosette *at all*. I'll be able to see him, you see. And he'll be able to tell me how things are, when he's older. And perhaps . . ." *And perhaps one day, he'll be able to come and live with me again.* The words had hung there, shining and unsaid, at the end of her sentence. It had seemed unkind to comment on the unlikeliness of this, so Margot hadn't.

And now it had all come true. A new husband, progressive enough to legitimize Robert. (How was Phyllis's mother explaining *that* to the neighbors? Margot wondered. Some tale of adoption, probably. It was easier for Phyllis, of course, as Robbie could presumably be passed off as a poor child of the parish in need of a home. Nobody would believe that of James. Could they perhaps pretend her mother was ill? Or that she and Harry couldn't have children? Would anyone believe it? And would it matter, if they were married and James were legitimized?)

Of course it would matter, she told herself furiously. *Of course the village would wonder, and gossip.* Her father had risked so much already to help her. His good name and reputation were essential if he were to do his job, this job that was his whole life. She couldn't bring this on his household. On Ruth and Ernest. On her mother and all her village friendships. On Harry's parents.

Could she?

For a long time, Margot had played various fantasies in the back of her head. Her mother dangerously ill, begging her to come home and be a mother to James. Or wounded, perhaps, in an accident—not seriously, but enough that something would have to be done about James. "Perhaps it's for the best if James comes to live with you . . ."

She had always known, of course, that this was a fantasy. But now she wondered . . . could it happen? Would people really accept it? It was dizzying.

A family, with James in it. A future. Could it happen after all?

A YOUNG MAN
AT CHURCH

———•••◦)◦(◦•••———

MARGOT HAD NEVER BEEN VERY RELIGIOUS, EVEN
as a child. "I don't think it's quite nice of God to know
what I'm thinking," she'd said to her father once, a
remark that had amused him greatly and gone down in
family history. Jocelyn and Stephen had always been the
devout ones, as children at least. (Was Stephen still? She
realized she didn't know. She must ask.) Ruth had always
been supremely logical, and demanded the same logic of
the scriptures:

"But *why* was it all right for Moses to drown the Egyp-
tians if killing is wrong?"

"But if Jesus could raise Lazarus, why didn't he raise
everybody?"

"But Daddy, *why?*"

Their father rather enjoyed such debates, though Ruth was often dissatisfied with his answers—his patient insistence that faith was about more than logic had never convinced her.

Ernest had accepted the Scriptures without much fuss or interest. God in His Heaven. Father in his pulpit. Nanny in the nursery, and sardines for tea. Ernest had never committed a sin much greater than getting mud on his nice coat.

Margot felt rather detached from religion now that she'd left the vicarage—but even she could feel her heart lift as the family walked down the street surrounded by the glory of church bells ringing out Christmas Day properly for the first time in five years. The War was over! Christ was born! And—oh!

There he was. Standing outside the church, deep in conversation with Mrs. FitzPatrick—one of Father's more intractable Churchy Ladies, a small, fierce woman in her early seventies, with something of the fighting dog about her—his dark head bent in apparent fascination, nodding away as though nothing could be more interesting than what she was saying. So Margot had been quite right about that, all those years ago. She watched him out of the corner of her eye, trying to pretend she hadn't noticed him, feeling herself go stiff and formal, like a little girl at a party in a smocked pinafore and *quite* the wrong dress.

Ruth hopped up and down beside her, tugging on her hand.

"Margot! Margot, look! There's Harry! Aren't you going to go and say hullo?"

"Hush!" said Margot.

Harry glanced up at the sound of Ruth's voice and caught Margot's eye. Her face flamed.

"Harry!" shouted Ruth, waving, and Mrs. FitzPatrick—curse her—stopped talking about the state of the graveyard or whatever it was she was blathering on about and looked at them with naked curiosity.

Harry nodded to Mrs. FitzPatrick and came over to them.

"Hullo, Ruth," he said.

"Hullo!" said Ruth. "Did you and Margot row? Ernest thought it would be ungentlemanly to tell what you said, which I think is jolly unfeeling of him. Margot wouldn't tell either, but you will, won't you?"

"Oh, Ruth, don't be such an ass," said Margot.

Harry grinned and said, "My apologies, Detective Inspector, but a gentleman never betrays the confidence of a lady."

They exchanged meaningful looks over the heads of Jocelyn and Ruth.

Margot: *I am sorry, you know.*

Harry: *I know. It's all right.*

"Come along, children, we'll be late!" Jocelyn sang, and they hurried into their pew. There they sat, watching as the choir came in singing "O Come, All Ye Faithful" in their red surplices. Margot, sitting by the pew door, had a perfect view of the nativity set, now with the baby Jesus lying in his manger.

For a long time, Margot had felt ashamed to come to church.

"You should ask God for forgiveness," her father had said to her, not unkindly—he was never unkind—but Margot had still come away with the sense that she was an unclean vessel whom only sincere repentance could cleanse. It made her hate the church and her father a little bit. And while she was truly sorry—oh God, was she sorry!—she had never gone down on her knees and asked for forgiveness. She had told herself this was because she didn't believe in fairy tales, but now she wondered. Had she perhaps thought she didn't *deserve* to be forgiven? Did she think that still?

She looked at the face of the Virgin Mary, bent over her sleeping child. Mary was an unmarried mother too, she supposed—at least, not exactly, but she very nearly could have been. She wondered if the busybodies had shaken their heads over birth dates and timings. No—of course not—Jesus had been born in Bethlehem, hadn't he? Still . . . she looked at the girl in the stable and wondered not for the first time what really happened that first Christmas.

So many families had secrets. You couldn't live in a vicarage and not know that. People were always coming to see her father in tears, respectable people in absolute devastation. Sometimes the children would find out the story later—a son killed in action, or the collapse of a family business. But more frequently, they would never know. The parishioner would straighten themselves out and get on with their ordinary lives, and the visit would never be mentioned again.

Margot looked around the bustling church, full to the rafters, of course. Rows and rows of scrubbed faces and Sunday frocks. *"Hosanna in excelsis!"* sang the choirboys.

All these people, clean and hopeful. Would she ever be part of their number again, or would she always be on the outside?

After the service, he came over to her.

"I bought you a present," he said quietly. "I wasn't sure if it was the right sort of thing to send, but . . . Well, anyway. Don't open it here."

He passed her a small parcel wrapped in pale blue tissue paper and tied with a satin ribbon. The whole thing looked most un-Harry-like. Perhaps the shop had wrapped it?

"Thank you," she said wonderingly.

He gave her a nod, said, "Well, then," and was gone.

A HUNDRED
YEARS AGO

SHE OPENED IT IN HER BEDROOM WHILE THE
others were washing for dinner. It was a small silver bracelet with little charms set all around it.

Threaded through the bracelet was a slip of paper. On
it was written:

I bought this for my girl in Calais, a hundred years ago.

There was no signature.

CRACKERS
AND CANDLES

◆━━◆━◆◆❯❮◆◆◆━◆━━◆

AND THEN THE CHRISTMAS DINNER, IN ALL ITS glory. Crackers, plum pudding, and a glass of white wine, one for Stephen and one, surprisingly, for Margot—she really *must* be an adult now. The vicarage doors were thrown open at Christmas to all the lonely souls of the parish, mostly elderly people: old women and a couple of bachelors. As an adolescent, she'd found them rather funny and somewhat pitiable. But now, as a lonely person herself, she could see the loveliness of her father's gift. She looked at the Churchy Lady opposite her—Miss Timpson, whose life seemed mainly devoted to the church choir and her cat. Were there love affairs and mistakes and secrets in Miss Timpson's life too? Had she ever loved anyone the way Margot had loved Harry?

The drama of this dinner table was Stephen, of course.

The Churchy Ladies twittered around him, saying how pleased they were to have him back, how proud his mother must be of him, how *hard* those Christmases had been with him away. Stephen bore this about as well as Margot would have.

"Well, I was conscripted, you see," he told Miss Timpson. "So I don't know that she's got much to be proud of—I didn't have a lot of choice in the matter."

"Oh, but we're so indebted to you brave boys—as a nation, I mean."

How they kept trotting out the same old bromides! And how threadbare they were becoming with age.

Stephen made a face. "I spent half my war driving an over-promoted general around the fortifications," he said. "I sometimes think it might have ended six months earlier if I'd driven him into a bloody ditch."

Miss Timpson looked shocked. Then, "Well, dear," she said, "we must all be very glad that you didn't. I can't think what your mother would have done!"

And Stephen, to his credit, allowed himself to laugh.

Ruth, Ernest, and James finished eating long before their parents and disappeared upstairs while the adults lingered over coffee. Occasionally, one or another child would reappear at the doorway to ask "Aren't you *finished?*"

"How can *anyone* take a hundred thousand million years

to eat a piece of plum pudding and drink a cup of coffee?"

James ran over to Margot's mother and climbed onto her knee.

"Mummy! Come!"

"In a minute, darling."

"Not a minute. *Now*."

He pressed his nose up against hers. "*Now*, Mummy! Christmas tree!"

Enough, Margot told herself, willing her body to unclench.

···· ◆)(◆ ····

THE TREE HAD ALWAYS BEEN MARGOT'S FAVORITE part of Christmas. It was decorated on Christmas morning by their mother, and the drawing room was strictly out of bounds until she had lit the candles. Then the gas was dimmed, and the door opened, and they were allowed to view it in all its beauty.

Of course she knew that it wasn't anything wonderful, really: a Norwegian spruce covered in cheap tinsel and tiny candles. Of course she knew that. Of *course* it wasn't worth all the ceremony the vicarage imbued it with, and yet, and yet . . .

When their mother opened the door and the children pushed through and gasped . . .

The little tree sat in the bay window, its candles glowing, the angel on the top with her china wings outstretched, the presents nestling in the branches and beneath it. Margot glanced at James. He was wriggling with excitement, his mouth open, and unaccountably her eyes filled with tears. It had been worth it, then, all those lonely days, if it meant there were still moments like this one.

She glanced across at Stephen and saw that he too was moved.

"Not so shabby," he said, and she nodded. Not so shabby.

After the tree, there were games—charades with the family dressing-up chest, twenty questions, and dictionary. Then presents.

Her present from her parents was a pair of dancing slippers for the Hendersons' ball and a little silver locket.

"Don't open it now," her mother said quickly.

"Why not?" said Ruth at once, and Doris said, "Them as ask no questions hear no lies," just like Nanny used to.

After the presents, there were carols around the tree, with Stephen on the piano. It was a hideously Victorian Christmas. But somehow because it was Father doing it and he really meant it, and because Mother was obviously so pleased to see Stephen at the piano again, in his old spot . . . Well, somehow it felt real.

She looked around the room—at the lonely people

singing away at their hymnbooks, at Ernest and Ruth still wearing the hats from their crackers, at James nearly asleep on her mother's lap. He had loved his ship. It was quite the nicest present he'd gotten, and she and he had played with it all afternoon.

She opened the locket, making sure that nobody but herself could see. Inside was a little photograph of James, his eyes wide, his head tipped to one side.

Perhaps it was a message. Perhaps her mother had seen that she and Harry were going to come to an arrangement, and perhaps this was her way of saying that she thought Margot should take James back. He was Margot's child, after all. Surely he would rather live with his real mother than grow up to find out that she had abandoned him? And after all, he must be a lot of work for a woman her mother's age. It wasn't like he would be moving to live with a stranger. He could still see her mother anytime he wanted to, of course he could.

A child ought to live with his parents. Oughtn't he?

MISTAKES

MAYBE IT HAD BEEN A MISTAKE TO GO TO DURHAM.
A mistake to leave James. Maybe Margot should have gone
home with her mother, pretended she'd come back to help
with the baby, stayed a part of his life. It wouldn't have
seemed so strange, with help so hard to find.

But she hadn't. She and James had stayed their four
weeks in the home, then James had gone back to the vicarage with Mother, and she—still bleeding, still finding it
painful to walk—had gone to the Boarding House for Young
Christian Ladies and a secretarial course in Durham.

The goodbye had been strange and rather forced. Her
father had come to escort Mother and James home, which
meant that her aunt had had to be drafted to escort Margot
to Durham. Margot understood all the reasons this was

necessary—James was so small, he and Mother had so much luggage, it would look so strange if Father had not been there to help them home. But she couldn't help feeling that she was being punished. That she was a problem that had now been solved, and everyone could forget about the whole ghastly affair and get on with their lives.

She said goodbye to James in the waiting room at the train station. It was three-quarters full of soldiers and sailors in uniform, ladies with shopping bags, and an elderly woman who kept coughing up phlegm into a handkerchief. Margot had felt sullen and cross and like she was going to be sick. Everyone had insisted on treating her as though she were a whiny child spoiling a day out. Her aunt and mother talked mostly to each other, while her father had busied himself with tickets and newsstands. James—little beast—had slept through the whole thing.

All the time they were waiting, Margot had been wondering if she would say something. Protest. Cry. Grab the perambulator and make a run for it.

But when it came to it, the scene was so wretchedly British and public that she had done nothing.

Father had said, "Well. We'd better make a move, then."

Her mother had embraced her and said, "Goodbye, darling. Send us a cable when you get there, will you?"

Margot had stared at James. She wanted to hold him,

kiss him, tell him she loved him, but he was sleeping so peacefully, and the waiting room was so public. What would he think when he woke up and she was gone? Would he miss her? Would he think she had abandoned him? She had been shamefully close to tears.

Her mother must have seen it, because she said briskly, "Come along, Andrew, we'll miss the train."

And they were gone.

Twenty minutes later, Margot and her aunt were on the train to Durham.

The Boarding House for Young Christian Ladies was an awful place. Everything was cheese-pared, from the individual pats of butter on the side of their plates to the coal for the fires in the communal areas. There was no privacy, and everyone was forever in one another's business. If you so much as wore a new blouse to dinner, it was commented on and dissected. The food was awful, even by wartime standards—watery cod and stewed prunes and tapioca pudding. In winter it was freezing, and in summer it was dreadfully hot. The other girls seemed impossibly young and silly. Had she ever been like that? It seemed incredible. She felt about a thousand years old.

It was ridiculous, Margot knew, to be stuck somewhere so third-formish. Probably she ought to go somewhere else—but the thought exhausted her. And how sickening if the somewhere else turned out to be just the same?

It was strange, though. She, who had always been so social, was so isolated now. You would have thought she would mind terribly, but she found herself struggling to care. She couldn't summon the energy to be interested in the other girls' petty dramas.

The work in the school was fine, if dull: typing letters to parents, sending out invoices, immersing herself in the day-to-day administration of a busy organization. Her mother had found the job for her, thinking it would be nice for her to be around girls nearly her own age, but in fact it was just depressing. These girls had their whole lives in front of them, while Margot couldn't help but feel as though hers was already over.

The topic of "spare women" was a common one in the boardinghouse. There was much talk about who would be married and who would not, and how to achieve this longed-for state. Margot found it hard to care. When they asked her about it, she said her fiancé was missing in action, and they treated her with the respect they gave everyone with a young man in the forces. But since losing James, she had found that even her feelings for Harry had been crushed. It was as though there was no space for anything in her head besides the grief that she felt for her baby. It consumed her. Harry—who had once felt like everything in the world—had been lost. She couldn't grieve for both of them. Instead she found herself furious at him. If he hadn't gone to France. If he hadn't been lost. She'd been sixteen, that last leave. A child. Shouldn't he have known better?

She thought of her father, who would never, in a million, million years, have ever put her mother at risk of such a thing happening. At fifteen, she had thought him the most incredible bore, but now . . .

She'd found it impossible to remember her love for Harry. All she could feel was the loss of that warm little body resting against her chest.

That baby who would grow up calling another woman "Mother."

What could anything mean, compared to that?

⎯⎯⎯◈⎯⎯⎯

The Vicarage Church Lane Thwaite
North Yorkshire
26th December 1919

Dear Harry,
Thank you so much for the lovely bracelet. It is very beautiful. I hope you had a lovely Christmas.
Yours,
Margot

Dear God, she sounded about seven years old! Those two lovelies were very bad style, she knew, but it would look worse to cross one out, and she was running out of writing paper. Boxing Day was always the day for thank-you letters in the vicarage. Could anything be less like a love letter?

———————————

5 Watery Lane Thwaite
North Yorkshire
26th December 1919

Dear Margot,

I bought it from a fellow who was rather down on his luck. He was trying to get back home to his wife and kids in the country. I thought you might like to think you'd helped a family reunite.

Talking of reuniting, we're holding a luncheon party on the 30th. Nothing fancy—food and fellowship from half twelve, maybe some cards, and games for the children. The invitation officially extends to you and Steve and Jocelyn and Ruth, but of course Ernest is welcome if he wants to come, though he'll be rather at the smaller end of the pack.

Mother is inviting all the parentals as well, so I'm not sure it will be quite the place for a heart-to-

heart, but—well, are you going to the Hendersons'
on the 31st? And if so, could we perhaps sit out a
dance or two? Your mother isn't planning on chaperoning, is she?

Yours,
Harry

⎯⎯◆⎯⎯

The *Vicarage* Church Lane Thwaite
North Yorkshire
27th December 1919

Dear Harry,

Thank you for the invitation. We'd all love to
come, including Mother, but not including Ernest, who
is going skating on the duck pond with some boys from
the village. And doesn't much like parties anyway.

Yes, I'm going to the Hendersons'. And no, Mother
isn't coming. That's a very good idea. I do honestly
want to tell you. It's just I didn't quite know how,
when there's always beastly chaperones about. And—
well, I'm so terribly afraid you'll hate me.

Yours,
Margot

5 *Watery Lane Thwaite*
North Yorkshire
27th December 1919

Dear Margot,
   I could never hate you.

                      Yours,
                      Harry

THREE DAYS

———•••••◦•◦≫≪•◦•••———

THREE DAYS: TWENTY-EIGHTH, TWENTY-NINTH, thirtieth of December (when she would see him again! Oh happy day!), and then it would be the thirty-first. The ball. She would tell him—she would have to tell him, wouldn't she? And then he would know.

And her whole fate would be decided.

The sense of foreboding reminded her of how she had felt the day the telegram came about Harry. How she had stood in the hallway with it, thinking of all the different futures it might contain—*wounded, missing, killed, maimed*—and how she would open it and then she would know. But at that moment, all those futures were still possible.

The vicarage had been full of people, she remembered. It had been blind luck that it had been she who opened the door and not Edith or Ruth. Her mother had a Girls' Friendly Society meeting in the drawing room, and Ruth and Ernest were sliding down the servants' stairs on tea trays (Nanny had given in her notice, and they had been left rather to their own devices). Edith was beating carpets in the garden and singing at the top of her voice (Margot could hear her when she opened the door to the telegram boy). There was even a clock-winder there in the hall.

"Everything all right, miss?" he'd said anxiously, seeing the little brown envelope in her hand.

She'd said, "Oh yes, I'm expecting a cable from my aunt," and had hurried upstairs before anyone else could find her.

The bedroom had been empty, thank God. She couldn't remember where Jocelyn had been. She had sat on the bed, wanting to wait a little longer but knowing from bitter experience how soon it would be before someone burst into the room demanding something. She had wanted—*needed*—to open the cable alone.

So in the end, she had rushed it, turning what ought to have been one of the most significant moments of her life into something hurried and furtive.

So sorry . . . missing in action.

It was from his mother. They were holidaying in the

Lakes. Who had told *them*? One of the servants, presumably. How wretched the whole thing was!

⋯⋯◆≫◆≪◆⋯⋯

SHE THOUGHT BACK NOW TO HER SIXTEEN-YEAR-old self, how happy that girl would have been to know that Harry was alive. Whatever future she was to live in, it was not one in which Harry had never come home. That was something to remember and be thankful for. If God gave her nothing else, that should be plenty.

But still, she wanted more.

A future with Harry. Or a future with Harry and James, somehow. Or a return to the dull misery of long afternoons alone in the office with her typewriter, of tapioca pudding and chilblains.

Once again, she held those separate futures in her hands, as she had held that small brown envelope. In three days, the envelope would be opened, and she would know. But for now, all three were still possible.

Sunday, and a surprise in the church—Harry Singer, sitting beside his mother in his old army greatcoat, holding the hymnbook, singing along with the best of them. She felt her mouth drop open. Was he there to see her? He must be, surely? Harry Singer, who never set foot in a church except under duress.

She stared and stared, drinking in the sight of him. He turned and smiled at her. It was such a lovely smile—so warm and delighted at her surprise. Harry Singer!

"Fancy meeting you here," she said to him afterward, over the tea and cookies.

"Well . . . I heard there might be other inducements," he said, and she felt herself go warm all over.

"Did you?" she said. "That'll be Edith's leftover Christmas cake, no doubt?"

"No doubt," he agreed with a wink.

·····•◆◆◆•·····

DRAMA IN THE EVENING. STEPHEN—WHO'D BEEN growing steadily more morose since Christmas—chose Sunday supper to announce that he was no longer in employment. Tears from their mother and a disappointed-but-not-exactly-surprised look from their father.

"But *why?*" their mother said.

Stephen shrugged. "Nothing seems to matter very much these days, does it?"

Poor darling Stephen. There had been months and months like that for her in the boardinghouse in Durham. It was a perfectly wretched sort of way to feel. But things had always mattered intensely to her mother, so she clearly found this incomprehensible.

Margot's mother snapped, "Oh, don't be ridiculous, Stephen! You're very lucky to have had such a good job at all! I know an office isn't as exciting as the Front Line—"

"Mother!" said Jocelyn.

Even Ruth knew that was the wrong thing to say. Stephen stood up, his narrow face flushed.

Margot's father said, "All right, my lad," and laid a hand on his arm. "Come on, now."

They disappeared off into his study and did not reappear until after Ruth and Ernest were in bed.

"Did he stick it to you?" Jocelyn asked, but Stephen just shrugged.

"Actually, he was pretty decent about it." He stretched his arms over his head. "I tell you one thing, though; that's the last time he's going to try and shove me into some ghastly office."

"So what *are* you going to do?" Margot asked, but Stephen didn't seem to know.

"We are a wretched lot, aren't we?" he said. "Poor old Mother and Father. And they had such high hopes for us all!"

ORDINARY THINGS

THE TWENTY-NINTH OF DECEMBER. MARGOT SPENT the morning playing with James and Doris—he *did* like her, now that the initial shyness had vanished. As much as he liked Jocelyn, at least, and more than Doris. He looked round eagerly when she came in, and sat on her lap while she read him storybooks, and . . . Oh! Wouldn't it, perhaps, have been better to have handed him over and never seen him again? At least then she could grieve. How could you grieve for someone who was running about like a little cherub in gingham rompers, shouting, "Book, Margot!" and waving *Cinderella* at her? What could you do with grief that had nowhere to go?

She didn't know the answer, so she took her restlessness to Mary's, where she found George on the hearth rug, mending a toy boat, the baby sleeping in her cradle, and Victoria out for a walk with the nursemaid.

Mary greeted her with tea and enthusiasm and listened patiently while Margot tried to explain all of this. Then she said, "Margot—you're allowed to be happy, you know. You didn't do anything wrong."

"Didn't I? I'm not sure Father would agree."

Mary dismissed that with a wave of her hand. "You're making yourself miserable," she said. "Because you think you don't deserve happiness. But who does that benefit? Not James. Certainly not your mother. You gave up James to give everyone a better life. So live yours. Otherwise what was the point?"

"That's all very well for you to say," said Margot, aggrieved. "What exactly do you want me to do with my life? It isn't as though I ever had a burning ambition to go onto the stage or anything. I just wanted—well, what everyone wants. A house and a family, ordinary things."

"And Harry," said Mary.

Margot didn't rise to that. "What I want," she said slowly, "is what you've got, really. Only with Harry and James, all nice and legal. But it's idiotic to think about it. I don't suppose Mother and Father would really let me take James away. They wouldn't, would they? And he's adopted now—I signed the filthy bit of paper myself. So . . ."

"Adopted?" George looked up from the boat.

"Yes. There was a fearful lot of beastly forms and things."

George said, "But I say, old girl. You do know adoption isn't legal, don't you?"

"I'm sorry?" Margot was startled.

"You can't just give a kid away like a piece of furniture. Not in this country at any rate."

"But . . ." Margot stared at him. "Hold up a minute. All the girls in the maternity home I was in—they had to sign these great long adoption forms giving their children away. They . . ."

"Absolute tosh. The home probably drew up the whole thing out of plain cloth."

"Golly," said Margot. She wasn't sure whether to giggle or cry. "Just think of all their lectures! Someone," she said with increasing confidence, "should write to the papers about it."

George waved a beatific hand. "Be my guest."

Margot was quiet. Then she said, "You mean . . . if I decide I want James back. If Harry and I . . . I mean . . . my parents couldn't—"

"Couldn't do a thing to stop you."

"Crikey."

Mary said, "But your mother . . ." Margot looked at

her, and she quailed. "I mean—well, she loves James, doesn't she?"

"She could still see him," Margot said. Mary raised her eyebrows. "She'd be happy for me," Margot said, but even to herself it sounded unlikely.

CHARLOTTE

———•··•≫⊱≪•··•———

JOCELYN WAS BRUSHING HER HAIR BEFORE BED. "Ninety-seven, ninety-eight, ninety-nine, and that's the hundred!"

"Jos?"

"Hmm?"

"Does Mother love James?"

Jocelyn put down her hairbrush and turned to look at her sister.

"What do you mean?"

"I mean—well—I know she wasn't exactly pleased about having him, and . . ."

"Margot, what are you talking about? Of course she loves him!"

"I know that, but—she's getting on, isn't she? She'll be forty-six in February. I thought . . ." She faltered. "What?"

"Margot, you can't be serious."

"I just—well, if Harry and I were to get married, and—Stop looking at me like that! She never wanted him in the first place!"

"Of course she didn't! You didn't either!"

"It wasn't that I didn't—"

"Oh, Margot, don't be absurd! Of course you didn't. You were hysterical. Don't pretend you weren't!"

Margot hesitated. *Was Jocelyn right? Of course she was right.*

"Even so—"

"And now that Harry Singer's come home, you think you can take James back like—like a parcel."

"He's not a parcel! He's my son!"

"Honestly, Margot! *How* you could do such a beastly thing to Mother, I can't think! After Charlotte and everything!"

Charlotte.

"All right!" said Margot. "I was only asking, that's all."

But Jocelyn, normally so calm and reasonable, was angrier than Margot had seen her in a long time. "Of all the selfish beasts," she said furiously. "You are the worst."

Margot flung herself onto the bed and turned off the light. She and Jocelyn lay in the dark, both fuming.

Charlotte.

····•◦❳❲◦•····

CHARLOTTE WAS MARGOT'S SISTER—HER *REAL* SISTER. She would be nearly four now, had she lived, but she hadn't—she'd lasted a week and then died. There had been something wrong with her—Margot was hazy about the details. She remembered the awfulness of it. It was January 1916, when the weather was icy, and news from the Front was bleak. Charlotte was supposed to be a spark of hope in a family that desperately needed it.

They'd had the news only a few weeks earlier that Margot's cousin John had been killed on maneuvers. (The idea had been to call the baby John, or Joan, in his honor, but that had had to be hastily reassessed when it became clear that Charlotte was not going to live.) Cook had given her notice just before Christmas, and with Mother so close to her lying-in, everyone else was forced to take up the slack. But the baby had been much longed for, much talked about and prepared for. Jocelyn and Margot and their mother had knitted little matinee jackets and booties. Ernest's old cradle, bath, and perambulator had been fetched out of the attic and dusted off. She had been the one true happy thing that awful winter.

When she died, it felt like the end of the world. Their mother had fallen into a deep depression, which had lasted for most of that year. That unhappiness at home had been the backdrop to Harry and his family's arrival, Margot remembered. It had been part of that whole reckless, unsettled summer.

And part of why she'd been so desperate to escape.

ONE DAY

————— ✦✦✦ —————

THE THIRTIETH OF DECEMBER. THE LUNCHEON party.

Harry.

The usual lovely chaos of his household—so familiar from the tea and tennis parties where they had first fallen in love. Games for the younger children—devil in the dark and blindman's bluff and sardines. Whist and bridge in the drawing room for the older set. (Stephen and Jocelyn disappeared into here with some relief—both were excellent cardplayers, and neither cared very much for socializing.) Cold meats and cheese and bread and fruit in the dining room, with potted shrimp and a box of crackers and a jar of olives and a big seed cake—oh, how glorious to have cake again! Oh, how she had missed it!

The parents—those who weren't supervising the children's games—all sat in the parlor, with the door open so they could see into the hall and up the stairs. It would be idiotic to try and sneak away, she saw at once, and Harry didn't even attempt it.

The rest of them, the lumpish, awkward young people that they were, neither one thing nor the other, all crowded into the hall and the dining room. Chairs had been brought down from the rest of the house and scattered about the place to accommodate this. How awkward it was and yet how nice too. How familiar. People she had known all her life, like Jack, Dickie, Betty, Annabel, Beryl, and Sue. Dickie had lost an ear and most of one hand on Hill 60. ("An *ear?*" said Harry. "Isn't a leg or something more traditional?") He was engaged to be married to Peggy, who was showing off her little sterling band with the paste diamond in it like it was the Koh-i-Noor. Jack was still in his uniform, grinning like an idiot at all the girls.

They looked, she supposed, like any other set of newly adult children. And yet what secrets did they all carry? What histories and heartaches? Why did Beryl look so shifty when Jack came into the room? Why did Harry's sister Mabel look so much like she was going to cry? What did all these people think about when they were alone in their rooms at night?

Who were they all *really?*

Harry.

Harry smiling at her when she came in the door, with a smile she was *sure* he kept only for her. Harry, so attentive—taking her coat, asking about her Christmas, fetching her a glass of lemonade, and laughing at her descriptions of the charades and the Lonely of the Parish. Harry, who made her shiver all over and—well, sort of come to attention when he was in the room. Harry, who promised so much—respectability (an awful word but an honest one), a home, a future, a family, an escape from the awfulness of damp boardinghouses and spats over who'd used the last of the hot water and who wasn't speaking to whom. A life with James.

Harry's house was very like her own: a noisy, shabby, chaotic kingdom. But the garden—thanks to Harry's mother—was really lovely. On the way back from the WC, Margot stopped at the window to admire it: the trees and the grass all dressed in frost, the high, rolling fields of the dales stretching out behind it. Say what you like about Thwaite, on a day like today, it was beautiful.

He came up beside her and leaned his face against the glass.

"Hullo!"

"Hullo." She smiled at him.

"We haven't managed to spend much time together, have we?" he said. "Do you remember, that summer . . . ? Every minute we weren't together was agony."

"Of course I remember."

"It seems so long ago, doesn't it?"

She looked at him. His long, kind face, the funny tuft at the back of his hair that he never managed to control.

"Not so very long," she said, though secretly she agreed with him. It felt like a thousand years ago.

He gave her that smile again. There was something about Harry's smile. Nobody else seemed to see it—perhaps they *didn't* see it—but the warmth that radiated from it was like a blazing fire on a cold day. She thought she could sit beside it and rest forever.

But could she ever really rest?

"It's funny . . ." he said, swinging the curtain cord absently, not looking at her. "Coming back, I mean. While you're out there . . . you feel so distant from the fellows at home. Like it's another world. And then when you're home, it doesn't go away, somehow. At least the chaps who were out in the trenches can talk to each other about it. I know it must have been hideous, but you do feel rather out of it if you were just a prisoner of war."

"What was it like?" said Margot, fascinated by this idea. "Really? Was it awful?"

"Oh . . ." He stared out the window at the garden. "Bits of it were fairly brutal. It's just . . . well . . . it's not really something you can talk about to anyone. It's frightfully romantic to have suffered in the trenches, but it's rather different when it's our own boys who were doing the blockading. There were times when I thought I hated our navy. There were children starving in Germany because of men like my cousins. How are you supposed to think about something like that? It doesn't tend to go down very well when you try and talk about it."

"No, I suppose it wouldn't." She didn't look at him. "Like a thicket between you and the rest of the world. Like everyone else can be happy . . . and normal . . . and you can't because you carry this awful weight around everywhere. And you can't ever put it down or talk about it, so you're always pretending to be something you aren't. And you know if people ever found out, they'd hate you. I think it must be rather like committing a murder or something. You couldn't ever forget it, could you? Or be happy again."

"Heavens!" He looked at her. "It isn't so bad as all that. Although I know some chaps at the Front have rather a horror show to carry. I got off lightly, really, compared to most."

She wondered if he was telling the truth. He'd been in that nursing home on the Isle of Wight for months. He must have had a pretty rotten time of it.

"Father once said," she said thoughtfully, "that it never does to compare your troubles to other people's. That grief is grief, and you can't know how heavy someone else's is unless you carry it. I mean, is it easier to lose your leg or your mind? Or your son? How can you compare them? And why would you? What difference does it make?"

"I think your pater's pretty wise, you know," Harry said.

She flicked her eyes across at him and saw that he was watching her with such warmth that she couldn't look away.

"What did happen to you, Margot?" he said quietly, and she blushed.

For the first time, she really felt as though she might be able to tell him.

"I . . ." she said.

They stared at each other. Then, from downstairs, they heard voices calling.

"Harry! Harry, you old devil, where are you?"

"Margot!"

"Dinnertime! Come on, chaps, come down!"

They grimaced at each other.

"Tomorrow," said Harry. He turned away and went downstairs.

SILK AND SCENT

———•∘⊷⊷∘⊷⊷∘•———

AND THEN THE THIRTY-FIRST ITSELF. THE DAY OF
Judgment. Margot and Jocelyn dressed for the ball.

"How lovely to be having balls again! Of course, before
the War, I only went to children's parties, but even so . . ."
Jocelyn's voice was rather wistful. "I suppose there are
heaps of dances in Durham."

"Not at all." Margot was brisk. "Not now, at any rate.
Last year was different, of course . . ."

What a strange time that had been! All the girls had
gone a little wild with the joy of it; the young men home
from the War, the peace here at last. Everyone giddy and
drunk with reaction. The celebrations in the streets. The
parties that lasted all night, the fierce urgency of the dancing and the drinking, the girls sneaking in through the

windows in the early hours of the morning. It had frightened Margot a little.

"Here," she said, changing the subject. "Let me finish buttoning you up— Stay still, can't you? There! What do you think?"

Jocelyn surveyed herself dubiously in the looking glass. The blue dress *did* fit her, more or less, though she would never look as well in it as Margot had. The three layers of woolly underwear necessary for a midwinter ball didn't much help. Poor old Jos.

Margot, in contrast, couldn't help but see how effective her new dress looked. She had eschewed their mother's suggestions and found a pattern in an old copy of *Vogue* hiding in the bowels of her childhood dressing table. The dress looked deceptively simple, but it was striking, and no one would guess that it had once been a cloak. Her blond hair was neat and sophisticated, with a black velvet rose—an unexpectedly perfect Christmas present from Stephen, how*ever* had he thought of it?—slid above her ear. Their mother had found a pair of Victorian jet earrings in an old jewelry box. They would have looked ridiculous on Jocelyn, but in Margot's small creamy ears they were charming. A strip of black velvet around her neck completed the ensemble.

"You'll always outshine me," Jocelyn said without

sadness. "No matter what I do. Next ball I'll go in tweeds and galoshes and a woolly jersey. At least I'll be warm and comfortable."

"Sounds like a jolly good idea to me," said Margot, frowning at her reflection in the looking glass. She had always cared so much about how she looked. She still went through all the routines, but since . . . since James, she had felt detached from it. It was as though there were an outside Margot, who looked as lovely as ever, and an inner, secret Margot, who tore at her hair and rent her clothing and wailed and gnashed her teeth. How strange to be two such separate people! Would they ever be reconciled? The quiet, composed Margot in the mirror seemed to live on another planet than the desperate Margot inside. "It's ridiculous really, to expect so much from a ball . . . and yet we do. Your coming-out ball, Jos. How do you feel?"

"Absurd," said Jocelyn grumpily. Then, seeing the concern in her sister's face, she smiled. "All right, a little excited. It's just as well I've resigned myself to being an old maid, for I'm sure no one will dance with me."

"Stephen will, at least," said Margot. "And Harry and George if I ask them."

"Oh goody," said Jocelyn. "You do know how to make a girl feel special, I don't say."

THROUGH
THE DARKNESS

————————◆❊◆————————

THE HENDERSONS LIVED IN A SMALL MANOR HOUSE
at the edge of the village. The two families had never been
close, but the Hendersons came to the church at Christmas, Easter, and Harvest Festival, and all of the children
had been christened and confirmed by Margot's father.
They did not come to the children's parties her father held
for the parishioners, but all the older Allen children had at
one time or another been invited to parties at the manor.
Once, when Margot was about nine, they'd been to tea
with the Henderson children, but it hadn't been a success.
Stephen fought with Marjorie Henderson and pushed her
into the mud, and they'd been sent home more or less in
disgrace.

For children's parties at the Hendersons', the Allens

had walked through the village with Nanny. Margot had always resented this, particularly in wet weather, when they would arrive in galoshes and mud-spattered stockings, and would have to retire to a drawing room to change. The other, wealthier children would come in carriages or—on one or two glamorous occasions—even in motorcars.

Now their father had a motorcar of his own—a black Model T, like half the village. He was to drive them there, and they were to call a taxi to collect them when the party finished, sometime in the early hours of the morning.

James was in bed, but Ernest and Ruth were allowed to stay up to see them go. They sat on the stairs in their pajamas and dressing gowns.

"Goodbye!" Ruth called, waving. "I hope you have a simply marvelous time!"

"Bring us back some cake!" called Ernest.

"And one of those little pencils from the dance program!" Ruth added.

"And one for me!"

"And some champagne!"

"That's enough," said Mother. "Goodbye, darlings. Have a lovely time."

But the children's excitement was catching. Even freezing in the little car, her black dress hidden under her wrap and several blankets, Margot could still feel it. A ball! A dance!

Harry.

"Excited?" their father said to Jocelyn.

"I might be if people would stop asking," she said.

Stephen grinned. Their father turned the car into the manor drive.

"Oh!" Jocelyn said. "Oh look!"

It did look lovely. Every window in the manor was blazing. Chinese lanterns had been hung from the trees and glowed pink and purple and cream among the bare branches. In the long window of the ballroom, the Christmas tree glowed with little red candles shining among the baubles. It brought back memories of children's parties in the manor: girls in white party dresses, colored sashes, and hair ribbons; party games in the garden; tea in the hall on long tables with white tablecloths. Trifle and jelly and angel bread and little triangular sandwiches. The agonizing consciousness of the wrongness of their dresses and the shabbiness of their birthday presents.

How long ago that all seemed.

And now here they were at the door. The footman was directing them upstairs—Margot and Jocelyn up one staircase, Stephen another. This was Mrs. Henderson's room, she realized, looking around it with frank curiosity: the dressing table, the four-poster bed, the long looking glass. It was all fiendishly neat, of course. Imagine asking ladies to leave their wraps in Mother and Father's room! Among the mess of Mother's old pots of cold cream and Father's parish magazines and James's wooden animals from the Noah's ark, the piles of books by the bed, and the ashtray full of Father's pipe ash.

She and Jocelyn took off their wraps and laid them on the bed. Then they stared into the looking glass, Jocelyn gloomily, Margot appraisingly. After a moment, she took out her powder compact and dusted her nose.

"Ready?" she said to Jocelyn.

And Jocelyn said glumly, "If I must, I suppose."

And they were off.

Off down the long wooden staircase, back down the wainscoted corridor. Imagine living in a house like this! It was Norman, someone had told her—at least the banqueting hall and the solar were. Other parts were later, and the garden, of course, was Victorian. But still! Margot had always thought that if she could live anywhere, she would have chosen the old manor, with its moat and its herb garden, its dark, shabby rooms and its wonderful scent of cool, dusty stone, green leaves, water in springtime, and old wood.

Stephen was waiting in the hallway, holding their dance

programs with—yes—the little pencils attached with lengths of silk cord (she must remember to bring one home to Ruth). There was a gaggle of girls in shot-silk dresses, talking excitedly. From the hall, Margot could hear music and voices.

Her heart was fluttering. Her entire future might be decided tonight! Although she supposed that could be true any day, whether one wanted it or not. Margot thought of all the things she might do if she chose—marry someone unsuitable, run away to Paris, join a convent. Announce to the whole party that James was her son.

It seemed like it was much easier to ruin a life than to build one.

Tonight I shall find Harry, she told herself. *For once in my life, I won't funk it. I'll tell him about James. The rest is in his hands.*

She could feel the nerves shivering down her arms and her legs. Her stomach churned.

It's your own silly fault, she said sternly. And then, remembering what Mary had said: *Do you want to spend the rest of your life in purgatory for one foolish mistake?*

INTO THE LIGHT

NOT A HUGE CROWD, BUT PRESUMABLY THERE would be more later. A few faces she recognized. A noisy group in really lovely clothes—a dark-haired woman in a dark green gown so beautiful it made her want to go over and stroke it—they must be the party staying at the house. A girl in a bright yellow dress—goodness, she looked a fright! Boys in army uniform. Men in hunting pinks.

Where *was* he?

"Right," said Jocelyn, looking down at her program. "Let's get one dance onto this thing, anyway. Then it won't look so wretched if anyone else asks. Which do you want, Stephen?"

"I'll have two," said Stephen with surprising generosity. "Let's see—how about two and eight? And what about you,

Margot? When shall I have you? Shall we say one, then we've got it out of the way early? I expect yours will fill up pretty sharpish, won't it?"

"It's all right; don't mind me," said Jocelyn. "It's only my first dance; there's no need to spare my feelings."

"All right, I won't. Do you girls want any punch? I warn you, I'm not spending the whole evening running about after you, so you might as well say yes."

"Yes, please," said Margot.

She looked around the room appraisingly. There was the usual shortage of men. The invitation had asked them to bring a male partner—easy enough, of course, since Stephen was home—but clearly not everyone had managed. She reminded herself to find George and make sure he asked Jocelyn to dance.

Dance one with Stephen. Perfectly pleasant—Stephen was a pretty decent dancer when he put his mind to it.

"I better go and cheer up Jos," he said as the number finished, leaving Margot standing there, looking around the room. Betty and Annabel—she should probably go and say hullo, she supposed. Mrs. Henderson, talking animatedly to a cluster of new arrivals—how *did* she do her hair like that? She must look when she got a bit closer. Mr. McNamara—

"Hullo."

A tap on her shoulder. She started. And there he was. Harry Singer. In full evening dress. Goodness, he did look nice! His easy confidence was a rarity in this room, she realized.

"Harry! You're looking rather dashing, I must say."

"So are you." His glance was openly admiring. "Your mother didn't make that, did she?"

"She did. It's not so dusty, is it?"

"You could do worse." He looked her up and down. "No, not too bad at all. Do you have any free, or have I come too late?"

"No, of course not."

He smiled at her, and she gazed frankly back, drinking in the simple pleasure of his easy happiness.

She displayed her dance card to him with a directness that would have appalled the *Woman's Weekly* articles on the subject of feminine coyness.

"You see. I am yours for the taking."

A quick flick of his eyes toward her, then down again. Three years ago, he would not have let that pass. He really was on his best behavior.

"Well, then . . ." He took out his pencil and scribbled something on her dance card. Quite a lot of somethings. "There you go. I must dash—I've sworn I'll dance with both my sisters, and there are a couple of other duties I must fulfill—the mater was very firm—but I think we might make something of the evening nonetheless."

He handed back the card and she looked at it—*with trembling hands*, said the *Girl's Own* serial writer in her head. But no, they were perfectly steady. He'd signed himself up for six dances, including number three—was that a good sign? Too presumptuous of him? Not presumptuous enough? She was trying to work out how pleased she ought to be, when he added, "We needn't dance them all, of course. We should sit out at least one, for the sake of the gossiping mamas, oughtn't we? And of course"—that smile was back—"alterations can be made at a later stage in the proceedings."

"Increases or decreases," she said, keeping her tone light to match his.

"As you say." He inclined his head and disappeared into the crowd, presumably in search of his sisters.

She stood there, smiling to herself. *It will be all right. It will. It must.* And then, *Oh lord, is anyone else going to ask me?*

But almost immediately: "Care to dance?"

It was Mr. Phillips. One of her father's curates—heavens! Still, he wasn't so bad-looking as all that, though he must be nearly *thirty*. And she felt suddenly that she would like to dance. The band was playing a brisk foxtrot.

"Thanks most awfully," she said. "I'd love to."

THE FIRST OF SIX DANCES

·····›)(‹·····

A BALL. A REAL, LIVE BALL. IT WAS RATHER GLORI-
ous, really, especially now that her card didn't look so
fearfully empty. After Mr. Phillips she was asked again, by
a shy-looking boy with a stutter from church who was evidently determined to Do His Duty.

She smiled as graciously as she could and said, "Of
course. I'm booked for number three, but how about number four? And could you possibly ask Jos as well? It's her
first ball, and I think she's a little windy about the whole
thing."

The boy gave her a shy smile and said he'd be very glad
to. And then there was Harry again.

"I believe the next dance is mine."

A waltz. Oh, how divine to be waltzing with Harry!

She could see others in the room watching her, wallflower heads bending close to whisper. Stephen grinned as they went past, and one of the Henderson girls scowled—was she *jealous*? No, surely not!

He was a good dancer. (Of *course* he was.)

"All the mamas in this room are talking about us," he said, leaning closer, and she giggled.

"Do you mind?"

"No, I rather like it. Let's give them something to talk about, shall we? Supposing we *were* still engaged—and I don't believe we ever broke it off officially, did we? What do you think of a farming life? Would you like it?"

"I'm not sure. I don't know much about what it would mean. Would I have to feed baby calves and so forth?"

"Well, you might. And help with the hay-making and all that. It's not an easy life. Everyone on a farm has to work pretty hard, especially in spring and summer. But it's a sociable one. My uncle's farm—where I'm living at the moment—there's all sorts of people there in the summer, laborers and hay-makers and milkmaids and so forth. It's rather jolly in summer. Of course, my aunt runs the household at the moment, but I think the idea is I might inherit when my uncle retires—if he's pleased with me, I mean, but he seems to be so far. You'd like my aunt—she's a frightful brick. And my cousins Jilly and Mary. They're the only ones left at home, but they're decent sorts. And of course there's always something going on—fairs and hunting and the Women's Institute and all that sort of thing. Do you hunt, Miss Allen?"

"Don't be an ass. You know I don't. I've never even ridden a horse, unless you count the donkeys at Scarborough. Do you?"

"Well—a little. They taught us riding in the army, and my uncle's a bit of a hunting fiend. It's not so dusty. But there's hunt balls and things if that's more your scene."

He seemed entirely genuine.

She said, "Can you picture me as a farmer's wife—honestly, Harry? Would I do all right?"

"I rather think you might. I don't say it's all jollification—this winter's been pretty dismal, though I wouldn't say the farmhouse is much icier than that vicarage of yours. And it's a decent life for children."

She drew in a little involuntary breath. He looked at her.

"Don't you want kids?"

"Yes! Oh yes. I want a big family. Lots and lots of babies. Don't you?"

"You know I do." He looked at her seriously. "I rather like the idea of making something good out of the mess our parents left us."

All at once it struck her—what she was giving him if she

told him. The awfulness of the last two years, the knowledge that her son wasn't her son, the tearing, desperate grief of it. That was what she was giving to Harry. She hadn't thought that a man would mind about it in the same way, had thought he would be angry or disgusted—but perhaps Harry really would care as much as she had?

Could they possibly live the straightforward, sunlit life he was offering her if that secret—that grief—was between them?

But how in heaven's name could they live it if she kept it to herself?

They danced the rest of the waltz in silence, and at the end of it, he said, "I'm supposed to take Prissy round the room now, but I'll see you later?"

She nodded, rather breathless, and he gave her a smart bow and headed off toward his sister.

Stephen was nowhere to be seen. Jocelyn—where was Jocelyn?—oh, there. She was talking very earnestly to a middle-aged woman with a close bob and a cigarillo. The woman was dressed in a dreadful black sheath of a dress, but Jocelyn was nodding her head furiously as she talked. She looked rather breathless. Margot was wondering what they were talking about, when: "Hullo, old thing!"

"Oh, George! How lovely to see you! Where have you been?"

"Acute appendicitis. Didn't expect to see you sitting one out."

"Not enough partners," said Margot briefly. "Which reminds me—you will ask Jos to dance, won't you?"

"With pleasure," said George. "And happy to do the same for you, if you really have some free? I'm not sure I can face being mobbed by all the mamas of Thwaite. The thing about being the local doctor, of course, is there are so dreadfully many people one doesn't need an introduction to. And one can't refuse without losing custom."

"All right."

They compared dance cards and settled on number five.

"Any go with the young man?"

"Not yet. We're going to thrash it all out later."

"Well—jolly good luck and all that. I'm off to get a drink. Cheerio!"

Dear old George. How she liked him. She wished Mary was here—but of course she couldn't leave the baby.

Oh criminy. How was she possibly going to do this?

A MINISTERING ANGEL

· · · ·✖· · · ·

A DANCE WITH THE BOY FROM SUNDAY SCHOOL. A dance with George. Harry blew her a kiss over his shoulder as he tangoed past. Afterward, feeling rather at a loss, she went looking for Jocelyn. She found her at the buffet, hovering by the punch. "Jos!"

"Oh! There you are! I was wondering."

"What have you been doing? I saw you talking to that old goat—you were looking at her like she was the Second Coming or something."

"She's not an old goat!" Jocelyn looked shocked. "She runs an orphanage." The expression on her face was almost dreamy. "It's in London—she's got fifty little children she rescued from the workhouse."

Margot thought of the woman with the long black

dress. An orphanage! What a dull, worthy sort of project! At the back of her mind, Margot had always suspected that a lot of the mother-and-baby-home babies ended up somewhere like that. It was all very well talking about loving couples desperate for a child, but the truth was that there were far more unwanted babies than there were childless young couples. The workhouses were full of them.

Jocelyn read Margot's expression with her usual speed and flushed.

"All right! You needn't be such a beast about it!"

"I didn't say a thing!"

"You didn't need to." It took a lot to upset Jocelyn, but the combination of the night's excitement and her usual poor opinion of herself seemed to have done it. "You've always thought everything I liked was perfectly dreary. You don't want to run an orphanage—fine! Don't! But what exactly do you expect me to do with myself? Stay at home and look after Mother and Father? Spend the rest of my life as a typist?"

"Like me, you mean?"

"Don't be absurd." Jocelyn was really angry now. "Of course you're going to marry one day, once you've gotten over your idiotic self-flagellation—"

"Self-flagellation!"

"I'm not going to marry, Margot," said Jocelyn. "At least—I must assume I won't. So what's left for me?"

She had a point; Margot had to admit it.

"So that's what you're going to do, then?" she said, a little sulkily. "Jocelyn Allen, Ministering Angel?"

"You needn't be such a cat," said Jocelyn. "It's good work. If not orphanages, then—I don't know—being a poor-law guardian, or . . . or something. I need some sort of job to do."

She glared at Margot. Margot was rather taken aback, and slightly ashamed. Jocelyn was right, of course. Without people trying to do some good in the world, children like Phyllis's Robert would end up in a workhouse. It didn't bear thinking about, really, when you looked at it like that.

Not quite knowing how to apologize, she said, "I think you'd be rather decent at running an orphanage."

"So do I," said Jocelyn. But her expression did not soften.

SUPPER

————— ›»◄‹ —————

ANOTHER DANCE WITH HARRY.

"I spread them out a bit on the old schedule so as to give me something to keep me going when I'm whirling Mother's friends' ghastly daughters around the room. I say, you really can dance, can't you? Did you know Basil Henderson said you were the prettiest girl in the village?"

Then a dance spent sitting on the stairs with two girls she knew from long-ago dancing classes and who, astonishingly, turned out to be at art school in Manchester and working as a games teacher, respectively.

Another with Harry.

"I put you down just before supper, so you'd have to go in with me. Wasn't I clever? Basil Henderson was right, you know."

A break for supper. She ate with Harry, Jos, and George, and it was perfectly lovely. No one worried about what to say, everyone was pleasant and interesting, nobody said idiotic things, and she could feel Harry and George liking each other and Jocelyn relaxing. Was this what being a grown-up might be like? Never having to spend time with bores again?

Stephen had disappeared into a gaggle of brother-officer types. A bit much to expect him to chaperone his sisters to supper, perhaps. He hovered briefly over the table with a whisky and soda in one hand.

"All right?"

"Perfectly, thanks, Steve."

"Jolly good." He stood there a little awkwardly. "The ices are rather decent—I'd try one if I were you."

"All right. Buzz off now, Steve; you know you want to."

The supper was wonderful, though. Ices, little cakes, and lobster patties. Margot gulped down a lemonade and felt better for it. A footman came round with tall thin glasses of champagne. Margot took one and looked at Jocelyn, daring her to protest. Jocelyn hesitated, then took one too, a little defiantly. It tasted just as delicious as Margot remembered. The last time she'd drunk champagne was when the War ended, and the headmistress had insisted. She wasn't a bad old bird, really.

The men were having the sort of conversation young men always seemed to be having these days. The War, the War, the War, endlessly circling and recircling.

"Those hospital trains! Three bunks high—and the smell! I had a chap in the bunk above me with dysentery. Who thought *that* was a good idea, I'll never know. *Not* how you want to be woken up at four in the morning when you've just had the first clear night's sleep in five days."

Laughter.

"There was a fellow in my battalion who used to sleep through a bombardment. Pull his cap down over his eyes and drop off there and then. Can you imagine!"

Scoffing and disbelief. "He must have been deaf!"

"Not a bit of it. Said he'd grown up next to an iron-works and could sleep through the Apocalypse if he had to. If you're dead, you're dead, he used to say, and there's nothing any of us can do about it. Sniper got him in the end, poor devil. Often think of him."

Murmurs. Then, "Any of you chaps remember old Edwards? Did you ever hear the story about him and the *boulanger*'s daughter? No? Well, what happened was, Edwards, you see . . ."

Margot caught Jocelyn's eye, and she went scarlet. It didn't sound at all like the sort of *boulanger*'s daughter story they'd covered in French class.

THE WALTZ

NUMBER NINE WAS THE BROTHER OF THE ART-
school girl, who trod on her toes. Number ten was Stephen,
then eleven, twelve, thirteen were *Harry, Harry, Harry.* He'd
made damn sure she couldn't funk it, then. She accepted
no more offers after this, telling anyone who asked that she
didn't know how late they would be staying.

Stephen was looking rather tight. He clutched her arm
and said, "All right, old girl? Jolly good party, eh? Hendersons know how to do a thing, don't they?"

"Yes," she said. Then . . . "Look here, Stephen, don't you
think you've had enough to drink?"

"Eh?" He looked at her a little blearily.

"Oh, Stephen." She suddenly wanted to cry. The Stephen
in her head was still the little boy who had given all the coins

in his money box to a beggar woman and cried because he didn't want to go back to school. The adolescent who had flown at the prefects in a rage because he'd discovered them beating a younger student for the fun of it.

What had happened to that child? Was it the War?

Or did this happen to everybody as they grew up?

Did people look at her and wonder what had happened to her?

He was frowning at her. "Don't . . ." he said.

"Don't what?"

"Don't look at me like that." He swayed, then, suddenly vehement, said, "I'm sick to fucking death of it! You might let a fellow breathe!"

"Stephen!" She was shocked.

He rubbed his hand across his face.

"I'm sorry," he said. "Sorry—you mustn't mind me, you know. I'm . . ." He was still swaying. "I'm too old for this," he said dazedly. "Lived too long."

He pushed his way past her and through the dancers. She watched him, her heart tugging at her, wondering if she should follow.

"Jilted already?" It was Harry.

"Only Stephen," she said, her eyes still on Stephen's retreating back. "He's tight, I think."

He looked at her in silent inquiry, and she spread her

arms in a gesture of surrender. What, after all, could she do about Stephen?

"Come on," he said. "Let's dance away our sorrows. I'm frightfully sorry I've been so taken up. You wouldn't believe the number of girls Mother made me promise to dance with. Thought I'd better get them out of the way. Still, I'm all yours now. Shall we?"

A polka. And then another waltz. Margot clung to him, trying to savor the moment, one last waltz with Harry Singer. If only it would never end! He seemed to catch something of her fervor, for he held her tightly and did not try to speak. The other dancers seemed to part before them, Margot Allen, the pretty vicar's daughter, looking particularly well tonight, and tall, dark Harry Singer clasping her in his arms once more.

It was nearly midnight. Soon it would be 1920. A new year. A new life.

The waltz finished. He held her hand and her eyes and said, "We can't funk it any longer, can we?"

She shook her head. It was time.

TRUTH

·····➤···➤◄···➤·····

"WHERE SHALL WE GO?" SHE SAID. "IS THERE ANY-where . . . private? Where we can't be overheard?"

There were couples all over the house—on the stairs, in the hallways, in several of the window seats and powder rooms and smoking rooms. Everywhere there were other people. And this wasn't a conversation that could be whispered.

"It's all right," said Harry. "We can go to Basil's dressing room—I cleared it with him. It's just up here."

"Goodness," said Margot. Basil Henderson was the eldest Henderson boy, and something of a grand figure in the village. She felt rather impressed.

They went up the old staircase. There were girls on the stairs laughing together, and yet another boy and a girl half-hidden behind the curtains. They passed a footman bus-ily engaged in emptying the overflowing ashtrays—he didn't blink as they went past; through the billiard room—four or five young men here, playing billiards and smoking, no won-der there were no partners downstairs!—along a corridor; and into a small room that smelled of old wood and hair oil. Harry flicked on the light switch and there they stood, look-ing at each other, aware all at once of their closeness.

It was very cold. She hugged herself, wishing she'd brought her wrap.

"Here." He took off his jacket and draped it around her shoulders. "Well," he said.

They stared at each other.

She opened her mouth. "I . . ." she said, and then she shut it.

Because how could she do it to him? Bad enough that she had to live with this. But to force the man she . . . the man she loved . . . to force him to share it? How could she? It was barbarous. Much better to leave him ignorant.

It wasn't as though she could take James away from her mother. She'd known it all along. Her mother, who'd been so good to her. Her mother, who'd lost one child already—to ask her to lose a second! And James. To take him away from his whole family . . . ?

How could she even think it?

Had she ever, really, thought it might be possible? And since it *wasn't* possible, she should let it lie. Let her mother be happy. Let James be happy. Let Harry be happy too. He'd get over her. The girl he'd loved when he was nineteen? It wasn't as though it would be exactly hard to find someone else.

She should let it go. She should let him go.

Anything else would be selfish.

"Margot?" he said, and she shook her head.

"I don't think I can," she whispered.

Harry reached over and took her hands very gently in his.

"Look here," he said. "I've something I want to say to you. I'm going to say it, and then if you don't want to answer, I suppose we really are done. But I want to say it first."

She nodded.

"There's something you're hiding from me," Harry said. "You said so yourself, and all these people keep hinting at it: Mary"—Mary!—"and Jocelyn, and your mother. They keep acting as though there's a perfectly rational reason for the way you're behaving, and I've only to wait until you tell me yourself and all will be clear. Well, Margot, I *have* waited. And it's driving me mad. Was there another man? Is that it? You said not, but . . . You can tell me, you know. I'm a man of the world. I just—"

"Oh no, no!" Margot cried. "There isn't anyone else—of

course there isn't. You're the only . . . it's only ever been . . ."

She stopped in confusion.

"But there's something," he said. "Isn't there?"

She twisted her head away.

"Tell me," he said. "Whatever it is, I can take it."

Tears started in her eyes and spilled down her cheeks.

He put his arms around her and held her. She buried her face against his chest, like James against her mother, and at this thought, the tears threatened to overwhelm her.

"Tell me," he said more quietly.

She pulled herself away so she could look at him properly.

"James," she said.

He stared at her, uncomprehending.

"James, my brother. Only he isn't my brother. He's my son." He was still staring. "He's your son."

His mouth opened.

"My God," he said quietly.

"Now can't you see?" she exclaimed. "How *could* I tell you? It's tearing me apart. I can't bear it. I can't . . . Oh!" She shook her head furiously. "What I would give to be a man—not to know—not to *have* to know. What good could it do to tell you?"

"What *good?*" he said, suddenly angry. "You were going to walk away from me forever—do I matter to you that little? I'm *nothing?*"

"Nothing? I was being *kind*," she said, realizing as she said it how ridiculous she sounded. "I was choosing . . . I was sacrificing my happiness to . . . to save you from *this*."

"Your happiness!" He looked as though he were going to shake her. "What about *my* happiness? My marriage? My future? You were going to let me think you'd found another man—because you thought it would save my *feelings*? I have a son—a two-year-old child—and you weren't even going to *tell* me!"

"I knew you'd be angry," said Margot. "I suppose you can't bear to look at me now, can you? A woman with an illegitimate child? He's your child too, as much as mine! Whatever sin I committed, you committed it too!"

"Don't be absurd." Was it her imagination, or was he rather more vehement than necessary? "I'm—well, dammit, it's a shock! You must see that? I—well, I'm insulted, I suppose. Do you really think so little of me?"

She looked down.

"It wasn't exactly that," she said. Shamed into honesty, she admitted: "I didn't know how to tell you . . . or if I even *wanted* to tell you. It's been so long . . . and I'm so different . . . and so are you. You are, aren't you?"

"I am."

There was a pause. She said, desperately trying to draw the conversation back onto her turf, "Don't you want to know about it? About . . . about what happened, and James, and everything?"

"Go on, then." His voice was hard.

"Harry—"

"Go on! You want to tell me, tell me! You can't expect me to be *pleased* about something like this, can you?"

"You're being unfair," she pleaded, and he, clearly knowing it but not yet able to admit it, said, "Well, go on, go on! Say what you want to say!"

She wanted more, but evidently she was not going to get it. So, stumblingly, she began to tell. About her parents, and the home. About having to leave school—and for the first time, she realized what a loss that had been. She had never expected to go to university or anything like that, but she had loved her school, and her friends, and being sprites in the school play, and walking down the high street of the little market town arm in arm, and sitting on the grass in summer, watching the hockey matches and making daisy chains. James's birth had taken all of that from her too. She barely spoke to any of her school friends now.

She told him—or tried to tell him—how awful it had been, how separate she had felt from everyone and everything.

"What did you expect me to do? I wanted to do what's

right for James, but I *don't know* what the right thing is. I feel like whatever I do, I'm letting someone down. I've spent two years worrying that I did this terrible thing, giving him up, but the more I think about it, the more I realize there *isn't* a right thing. Whatever choice I made, I was going to hurt someone."

This at least he seemed to understand.

"How do you think I feel?" he said. "What the blazes am I supposed to do now? Should I—I mean, does your father want money? God! They must hate me."

"Oh no!" she cried. "No, they don't at all." Was that a lie? "And you mustn't try and pay them off; it wasn't like that. They—they think of James as quite their own, you see. They wouldn't—wouldn't want to confuse that."

"I see."

She looked at him rather sadly.

"You told me you could never hate me," she said. "But you do. I knew you would."

"Hate you!" he said. "You think this is hate?"

In the ballroom below, the music had stopped—she wondered vaguely why. She was aware, suddenly, of how close he was to her, together and alone in the small room. She felt his presence like electricity on her skin.

"Then what is it?" she said. "You don't still want me? After all this?"

He did not answer. Instead, he bent and kissed her, on the lips.

"I don't know what I want," he said. "But I know I've never loved anybody the way I love you. And right now, I can't imagine I ever will."

In the village, the church clock began to chime the hour.

Dong, dong . . .

Below them, voices were shouting.

"Happy new year!"

"Happy nineteen twenty!"

He pulled away and looked at her. "It's the new year," he murmured.

She closed her eyes. His lips on hers again. Her lips on his.

THE REVEREND

A RESTLESS NIGHT. OLD DREAMS. THE ONE WHERE she'd lost the baby—she'd put him down only for a moment and now he was gone and she couldn't find him anywhere. She was never going to find him. He was lost forever, but she couldn't stop searching. She woke early and lay in her bed, listening to the rain falling outside the window. Her room was above the kitchen, and she could hear Edith clattering about downstairs, baking the bread, beginning the day.

She had told him. And he still loved her. But . . . what did that mean?

What happened now?

A new life? A room in a busy farmhouse somewhere up on the dales? Fresh milk in the morning, and eggs for break-fast, and little children who looked like James jumping on haystacks, and fishing for frogs, and feeding the calves in the spring? Geese—could they keep geese? And goats. James would love a baby goat.

But James wouldn't be there. *Harry will be*, she told herself, trying to find comfort in this. *And we'll have children, lots of them. And I won't be lonely. And perhaps Mother might let James come and stay for the holidays.*

But did Harry still want that? She didn't know. He hadn't said he wanted to marry her, after all. You could love somebody and not want to be with them. Would she want to be with Harry if he'd done something like that to her?

As she lay wondering, she heard the creak of her father's door across the landing and the soft tread of his feet down the stairs. Her father always woke up early. He said the half an hour before breakfast was the only time he had to himself all day. He sat in his icy little study, praying and reading the Bible, readying himself to face the troubles of the world.

As children, they'd always been told never to disturb him, and normally Margot wouldn't have dreamed of it, but these were not normal times . . .

Surely he would let her speak to him? She felt suddenly that she must have this conversation now, or it would be too late.

She fumbled in the early-morning dark for the matches, struck one, and lit the candle. By the light of the candle flame, she lit the gas and dimmed the jet so as not to wake Jocelyn. Then, without bothering to wash (Edith had not brought the hot water yet, of course), she dressed herself—goodness, it was cold!—and slipped on her shoes.

The gas in the hallway was already lit. She padded downstairs as quietly as she could and knocked on the study door.

"Come in."

He was sitting at his desk, the Bible open on his knee. He looked, in the early-morning darkness, rather small and faded and, yes, old. He was a grandfather now. His hair was thin and pale.

"I'm sorry," she said. "I didn't mean . . . I just . . . I wanted . . ."

"It's quite all right." He motioned to the other seat. She felt suddenly as though she were in a headmistress's office, about to be given a dressing-down for talking to a boy on the way home from prep.

He watched her with an expression she recognized from his dealings with parishioners but had never seen directed at her before. A sort of expectant waiting. It made her strangely angry.

"I told Harry about James," she said abruptly.

"And?"

And how could she repeat that conversation for him?

"It's complicated. But—well. I think he still likes me."

"And is he going to marry you?"

Always the vicar. Why did it still come down to this? A ring or no ring. Why did it matter so much?

"I don't know. He's— It was rather a shock."

"Naturally. Still, he's a reasonable young man. One hopes that when he's had some time to think about it . . ."

"You want me to marry him?" Margot was surprised. "I thought you hated him."

"I try not to hate anybody," the vicar said. "But, naturally, when you were so young . . . You can't blame us for being angry."

She felt her hackles rising.

"All right!" she said. "Can we not do this? I know we were idiotic, but you don't know what it was like. Him going off to the War and—"

"Really, Margot." Her father looked almost amused. "I don't know why everyone assumes vicars are so unworldly. I spend my life counseling the despairing and the miserable. I do know what lust is."

Margot goggled. He had five children, of course, but still . . . !

"You weren't the first children to behave like fools, and

you won't be the last," her father said. "But thousands of young people faced the same test and came through with honor."

Oh God.

"Damn you!" she said, suddenly furious. "Damn you, damn you! Do you think I don't know that? Do you think I haven't suffered for it? I gave up my *baby*. When I think of the life he should have had—if only we'd married, if only he could have been mine—honestly. One day he'll find out that his mother gave him up, and I'll never forgive myself for it. Never!"

If her father was shocked, he didn't say so. He kept watching her with the same level expression.

"God can forgive much greater sins than that," he said.

For some reason this infuriated Margot even more.

"Just stop it!" she cried. "Stop treating me like one of your parishioners! I'm your daughter! And you just—just sit there and let Mother decide everything. And you never talk to me, and—I thought you were supposed to be so good at these sorts of things! You're rotten at it!"

Her father stared at her. Then he took off his spectacles and rubbed his eyes.

"You're quite right," he said.

"Oh no . . ." said Margot, shocked. She couldn't be right. Children weren't right.

Except she wasn't a child.

"When it comes to my own son and daughter, I am, it turns out, completely at a loss." He gave her a weary smile. "It seems my advice is much easier to give out than to follow."

"Why?" said Margot. "What advice would you have given yourself?"

He spread his hands.

"Oh . . . talk to your children. Forgive them. Recognize that this war has made a mess of their lives, and they're doing better than most at finding their way through it."

"Not me," said Margot. "I could hardly be doing much worse if I tried."

"You made a mistake," her father said. "And you've spent the last two years trying to put it right. You did what was best for James. You couldn't do any better than that."

She felt the tears start in her eyes.

"And do you—" She stopped, then started again. "Do you forgive me?"

He avoided her eye.

"For a long time, I couldn't," he said. "I tried. I prayed about you and Harry every day . . . but I was so angry. At what he'd done to you, and what you'd done to yourself. And James."

How like her father. He didn't pull his punches. But

how strange to think of him sitting in this cold little room, praying every morning for the ability to forgive the boy who'd made such a crock of his daughter's life.

"But lately . . ." He looked up and smiled at her. "James is such a blessing to us, Margot. I've always believed that God has His plan for us, and I've never been surer of it than now. James came to us just when we needed him the most. I expect it's selfish of me, but I'm grateful that he did."

Margot stared. This way of looking at the situation was an entirely new one to her.

"Would you like me to pray with you?" he asked. Her horror must have shown on her face, because he laughed. "Or not. You have my forgiveness, Margot, for what it's worth. I can only hope that one day I may have yours."

A WOODEN HORSE

"DORIS, COULD YOU GO AND SEE MOTHER FOR A minute, please? She wants to talk to you about some new clothes for Jamie."

"Of course, miss."

Goodness, what an idiotic girl! Could Mother really have found no one better?

"We'll keep an eye on James for you."

"Very good, miss."

James was riding his wooden horse, an ill-favored creature on wheels. It had been ridden at one time or another by all the vicarage children and was missing its reins and half its tail. He seemed completely indifferent to Margot and Harry.

Harry glanced at Margot, then at the child. "Hullo,

James," he said. "I'm . . ." He faltered. "What the devil am I supposed to say?"

"This is Harry, Jamie-o," said Margot.

James gave Harry a brief look.

"Trot-trot, trot-trot!" he said, pulling on the horse's mane.

"He doesn't care for me at all," said Harry, rather bewildered.

"Why should he?" said Margot. "He's barely met you. He'll like you when he knows you better."

"If you say so." Now the bewilderment was coming out as contrariness. "Is he happy?" he said abruptly.

"Yes, of course," said Margot. She put her hand on Harry's arm. "He's a very happy child."

He shook her off.

"Dash it, Margot," he said. "It's a pretty rum situation to find oneself in. A son! I have a son! I can't . . ." He shook his head. "Well. This is going to take some getting used to, that's all."

"I know," said Margot sadly. "It doesn't get any easier as it goes along. If anything, it rather gets more complicated."

"I just can't make sense of it," he said. "I'm damned if I know what to do. If I'm supposed to be angry—or—or I don't know. I was going to ask you to marry me . . ."

"But now you don't want that."

"I didn't say that!" he protested. "Dammit, Margot. You're the best thing that ever happened to me. I just . . . I need some time, that's all. Time to work out how the blazes I'm supposed to feel about this." And then, seeing her face: "I'm sorry," he said helplessly. "I'm being a brute, I know."

"A little bit."

"And I can't imagine what it must have been like for you."

At even this small kindness, her eyes filled with tears. She wiped them away with the heel of her hand. "It was the worst thing I ever did," she said. "Or the best. I don't know. Maybe it's both. Is that possible?"

"Blowed if I know," said Harry.

She gave a little laugh. James looked up from his horse in surprise.

They sat in silence for a long moment. Then: "Why don't we start again?" Harry said. "We made rather a mess of it last night, didn't we? Tell me everything you want to say. I'll listen properly this time, I promise."

"From the beginning?"

"From the beginning."

So she did.

ON THE NECESSITY
OF HAPPINESS

———————•❊•———————

"DID YOU EVER STOP MINDING?" MARGOT HAD
asked her mother, once. "About Charlotte, I mean?"

Her mother had shaken her head.

"You never stop minding," she'd said. "You just learn to
live with the space where they used to be."

To live with the space where they used to be. Was that
even possible?

But it had to be possible. Because one day, in ten years'
time, or fifteen, or twenty, or thirty, James would find his
birth certificate. One day he would read it, and on it would
be her name.

What would he think when that day came? Would he
be horrified? Betrayed? Disappointed? Or—was it possible—
might he be pleased?

She couldn't be his mother. He had one of those already. All she could do now was be the best sister and friend he could wish for, the best *person* she could possibly be. She must put aside her grief and devote her energy to being busy and happy, to loving Harry and any children they might have—surely they would have children?—to making a home so warm and welcoming that James would beg to spend his summers there.

She couldn't be his mother. So she must build the best life for herself that she possibly could and keep a space waiting for him in it. So that when he found out who she really was, he would not be ashamed, but proud.

TOWERS

· · ·◦▸◀◦· · ·

SHE WENT BACK UP TO THE NURSERY. DORIS WAS
sitting on the chair by the fireplace, darning James's night-
shirt. She looked up as Margot came in, and her face
brightened.

"Oh, miss! You couldn't sit with James for another
minute, could you? Edith's been most particular about me
bringing his tea things down, and it's that hard to find a
minute. I don't like to leave him, not since that time he fell
off the window seat, and madam was that upset—I wouldn't
be a minute, miss."

"Of course," said Margot. "I don't mind a bit. Take as
long as you like."

"Thanks ever so," said Doris, and she put down her
sewing.

James was building a tower, she saw, remembering the many similar towers built by Ruth and Ernest with the same box of bricks. You built them up and then you knocked them down; that was the game. Except James didn't like to knock his towers down. He simply built them, and admired them, and expected them to stand forever in the most inconvenient places, like right in front of the ash box.

This tower, Margot could see, was already looking precarious. James picked up a new brick and balanced it carefully on the top of the stack. It was a sloped brick, like half a roof. She watched with interest, wondering if the tower was finished, but apparently not. He took another brick and made as though to place it on the top.

Seeing disaster looming, Margot said, "No, don't do that. It won't balance on a slope—see? Why don't you lie that sloped brick on its side—like this, look?"

She half-expected either protest or interest, but he just said, "Yes!" and went back to hunting in the box.

"James," she said suddenly, and he looked up. "I do love you very much." It seemed an absurd thing to say, a gross simplification of all that she felt for this sturdy fair person in gingham rompers and red-button shoes. She remembered as a child kneeling on the window seat in this very nursery, reciting the list of people she loved to Nanny—Mummy and Daddy and Nanny and Stephen and Baby (that was Jocelyn) and Eliza (the maid) and Snuffles (the rabbit) and Agatha (the lady who ran the Sunday school) and Jane (her best friend at the time). Did love mean anything to James?

He nodded. "Love you, Margot," he said, and put his arms around her, burying his face in her stomach. She held him as long as she dared, then released him before he grew afraid.

I'll have others, she told herself, willing herself not to cry, wondering how anyone could ever have thought that a comfort. No matter what other babies she had, none of them would be *this* one, this vivid, clever child bending his head over his bricks, going through his solemn, contented little life without her.

Soon Doris would be coming up the stairs to relieve her. Soon she would have to leave him and go down.

Enough, she told herself. *Enough, enough.* She picked up a brick and bent back to the tower.

AFTERWARD

·····••·◆··•·····

AND AFTERWARD?

There is a house on a green hill, and a field full of wildflowers and cow parsley and long grass ready for the hay-making. There is an oak tree blowing in the wind, the branches making dappled shadows on the sward. There are the hay-makers coming down from the village with scythes over their shoulders, and the hay cart full of women and children with pots of ale and bottles of water and sandwiches in greaseproof paper parcels.

There are mice in the long grass, and frogs in the pools, and birds in the treetops, singing love songs to the morning.

There is a mother who holds her baby a little too tightly.

There is a little boy with fair hair running down the hill, knocking at the thistle heads with a hazel switch.

There is happiness, of a sort. Hold on to it.

Who knows when it will come again?

HISTORICAL NOTE

————————— ••◦•• ❭❭❬❬ ••◦•• —————————

THERE REALLY WAS NO WAY TO LEGALLY ADOPT A child in Britain until the Adoption of Children Act of 1926. Except in cases of neglect, the mother always retained parental responsibility and could, in theory at least, take back her child whenever she chose. Sadly, mothers were very rarely aware of this, and mother-and-baby homes and adoption agencies often took advantage of their ignorance.

The birth certificate with Margot's name on it was a wonderful plot device for me as an author, but there are many documented cases of adults finding out their true parentage only after everyone involved was dead, often when clearing out their parents' houses.

The First World War (1914–1918) was an enormously traumatic event for British society. American losses totaled around 117,000 deaths, almost all soldiers. Britain and Ireland, with a population less than half the size, lost approximately 1,350,000 people, many of whom were civilians. These casualties tended to be young people around Margot's age or slightly older, and those numbers do not include those who were injured or psychologically hurt. They also do not include the estimated 228,000 people who died in the 1918 Spanish flu pandemic. Literature from the twenties gives the sense of an entire society trying and failing to move on from this trauma, both collectively and individually. There was a stark divide between those who lived through the War—like Stephen and Harry and, to a lesser extent, Margot—and those who just escaped it, like Jocelyn, Ruth, and Ernest. George Orwell writes of his cynicism and boredom as a teenager at Eton, listening to adults lecture about honor and duty. And then later, as a young adult, finding himself surrounded by older men whose conversations, like the men's conversation at the ball, cannot leave the War alone, and realizing that he has missed out on something both terrible and defining.

Rights for women were also in a state of flux in this period. Women in Britain gained limited voting rights in 1918, and there is a sense in contemporary writing that young women were eager for more freedoms and opportunities, particularly the two million "spare women," who would never now find a husband. (Men were lost not just to the battlefields but also to opportunities in far-flung parts of the Empire.) Women of this period were still unable to graduate from most universities (Cambridge allowed this only in 1948) or work in many professions. Landlords were wary about renting to single women, and banks did not like to grant a mortgage without a male guarantor. The postwar generation of unmarried women was a transformative influence on British society, and their impact can still be felt today. Some of my favorite heroines in literature—from Harriet Vane in the Lord Peter Wimsey novels to Sarah Burton in Winifred Holtby's *South Riding*—are women like this.

ACKNOWLEDGMENTS

THANKS MUST START WITH MY EDITOR, CHARLIE
Sheppard, whose idea this book was. It has, as ever, been
an absolute joy to work with you. Thanks also to everyone at Andersen Press, particularly Paul Black and Chloe
Sackur. I am grateful every day to be published by you.

As usual, I read too many books to count while research-
ing this novel. However, special mention must go to Noel
Streatfeild's *A Vicarage Family*, Rosamond Lehmann's *Invitation to the Waltz*, and Elizabeth Cambridge's *Hostages to
Fortune*. Fans of these books will certainly recognize many
borrowings in this work. Also to Merry Bloch Jones's *Birth-
mothers* for an exploration of the trauma of giving up a child
for adoption.

This book was written while raising a young family—thanks go, as ever, to Tom Nicholls for continued support, child-wrangling, and for all the times you said "yes." Thanks to my babysitters, to writer friends on- and offline, and to everyone who continues to buy, read, and champion my books. You make this whole crazy business worth it.

ABOUT THE AUTHOR

SALLY NICHOLLS is an award-winning author whose first novel, *Ways to Live Forever*, won the Waterstones Children's Book Prize. She has been short-listed for the *Guardian* Children's Fiction Prize, the Costa Children's Book Award, and twice for the Carnegie Medal. She lives in Oxford, England, with her family.